YO-CAE-764

THE
CATHOLIC
CHURCH

THE CATHOLIC CHURCH

Barrie Ruth Straus

HIPPOCRENE BOOKS
New York

For information, address:
HIPPOCRENE BOOKS, INC.
171 Madison Avenue
New York, NY 10016

ISBN 0-87052-312-0 *hardcover*
ISBN 0-7818-0070-6 *paperback*

Library of Congress Cataloging-in-Publication Data available

Printed in the United States of America

M 9 8 7 6 5 4 3 2 1

Contents

Introduction

WHAT DO WE MEAN BY "THE CATHOLIC CHURCH" AND
what is its significance for contemporary society?

When most people talk about "the Catholic Church"
they mean the Roman Catholic Church. The Church
that we know today is a highly developed organization
with a uniform system of beliefs, practices, and rituals.
Together with the Protestant and Eastern Orthodox
Churches, this Church is one of the three main
branches of Christianity, but there was a time when all
three branches were part of the same Catholic Church.
The Eastern Orthodox Church separated from the original Church only in the eleventh century and the Protestant Church did not break away until five hundred
years later. The Roman Catholic Church traces its own
beginning to the apostles of Christ in the first century.
In fact, in those beginnings the Catholic Church could
be called a Jewish sect. We can see, then, how appropriate the term "catholic," from the Greek *katholikos*
meaning "universal," is.

Today the Catholic Church is changing in new ways.
These changes are more readily understood in the con-

text of the earlier changes. How and why did those changes occur? This book will tell that story.

The history of the transformation of a first-century Jewish sect into a medieval world power and then into the Catholic Church we know today is important beyond the history of Catholicism or even of the Christian religions. The story of the interaction between the Church and the world around it will show how Roman Catholicism has helped shape the life, thought, and art of contemporary institutions. These institutions are an important part of the Western culture that touches us all—regardless of whether or not we are Catholics or even Christians.

I

The Early Church from Jerusalem to Rome

Christianity and Jerusalem: The Underground Church

THE HISTORY OF THE CATHOLIC CHURCH BEGINS IN THE first century with the emergence of Christianity in the Eastern Mediterranean area of Asia Minor. The Catholic Church developed slowly and imperceptibly out of the early Christian movement whose roots were in Judaism. The first Catholics then were Jews living under the foreign rule of the Roman Empire. Because Catholicism

developed from the Judaism of this time, it is important
to understand what it meant to be a first-century Jew.
An earlier migration in 586 B.C., called the Dispersion,
scattered Jewish communities throughout the Mediterranean from Cadiz to the Crimea. By the time of the
Christian era approximately a million Jews lived in
Alexandria and Egypt, while Rome had a large enough
Jewish population to support a dozen houses of worship. Most Jews, however, lived in their ancient homeland, Palestine, which was divided into the provinces
of Galilee and Samaria to the north, Judaea and Idu-
maea to the south, and Peraea to the east.

Wherever they lived, however, Jews were united by
their shared belief in one God and their dedication to
the law, or Torah, and to the preservation of the Temple
at Jerusalem. As the central place of worship historically dedicated to God, the Temple was so much the
symbolic heart of Jewish life that most Jews would send
support for its upkeep as well as make frequent pil-
grimages to Jerusalem to renew their spiritual ties.

Whether the Jews lived in Palestine or throughout the
Roman Empire, their beliefs and practices were different from the predominantly Roman culture of their
rulers and neighbors. A crucial distinction was the
Jews' central belief in exclusive devotion to one God as
opposed to the many Roman deities. The Jews' relationship to this God was unique; they felt that God had
made a covenant, or pact, with Abraham indicating that
they were specially chosen, on the basis not of their
merit, but of God's inscrutable Will. This Will was revealed to the Jews through the Law, or Torah, handed
down from God to Moses on Mt. Sinai.

The centrality of the Law to Jewish life stemmed from

the Jews' belief that they had to lead a daily life that gave proof that they understood and were worthy of the honor God bestowed. This meant daily study of the Law in order to discover God's Will. But knowing that Will was not enough. At the heart of Judaic belief is the need to incorporate God's Will into each aspect of everyday existence. The result is that many acts which distinguish the Jews from others serve as daily reminders and evidence of their special relationship with God. Thus, circumcision, which made Jewish males distinctive from Gentiles, was both a reminder of the covenant and a mark of acceptance of the beliefs and practices of Judaism.

Jewish daily practices included not only praying, keeping the Sabbath and other Holy Days, and refraining from worshiping pagan gods, but also observing rules and prohibitions about food. While these practices gave the Jews a sense of belonging to a community no matter how far apart they might live, their customs also established the Jews as a group set apart from others. The Romans often misunderstood these strange customs. Because of the Jews' nonparticipation in pagan religious cults and their inability to share a meal prepared by pagans, Jews were often simply considered antisocial. On the other hand, many pagans admired the emphasis Jews placed on combining religion with morality, on charity and the family, and felt that Jewish separateness involved respect for pagan tradition as well as their own.

First-century Judaism included different opinions about what was most important to maintain the distinctively Jewish way of life, and especially to preserve it from foreign influence. The Sadducees and Pharisees represented mainstreams of thought, while minority views included those of the Zealots, the Essenes, and the early Christians. All points of view were considered equally religious.

The Sadducees emphasized preserving the purity of the past. They came mainly from prominent and aristocratic families. Many of them were powerful priests in control of the rites of the Temple in Jerusalem. They emphasized the sacred nature of Mosaic Law, and the need to maintain that law strictly, exclusively, and close to its original form. Throughout the years, many priests and scholars had written down different interpretations of the meaning of the Law, and of the way the Law could be adapted to contemporary life. The Sadducees, however, rejected this tradition of scribal interpretation as unnecessary post-Mosaic innovation. In this they differed from the Pharisees.

The Pharisees, associated with more widespread middle-class support, were religious leaders in control of the synagogues, local houses of worship that sprang up in the areas beyond the Temple in Jerusalem. Their answer to resisting foreign influence on Judaism was to apply the Law to the most minute aspects of daily life. For this reason, unlike the Sadducees, they were willing to adapt old Laws to new and changing situations. Consequently, they accepted the tradition of scribal interpretation the Sadducees rejected. The Pharisees also accepted the concept of resurrection, an idea which entered Jewish tradition around the second century B.C., after the time of Moses. On the other hand, the Sadducees rejected this concept. Acceptance or rejection of resurrection, then, was not fundamental to Judaism; however, its acceptance became the distinctive basis for Christianity.

The mainstream Judaism of the Sadducees and Pharisees focused on an acceptance of the joys of this world, and placed a high value on marriage and the family. In contrast were the beliefs of the Essenes, a comparatively small and radical group of about 4,000 Jews. They rejected the traditional values associated with the priesthood and the Temple in Jerusalem, and with ordinary city and family life. Despising wealth and private property and seeing pleasure as something to be avoided, the Essenes retreated to form a small, separate, ascetic, exclusively male community on the edge of the Dead Sea. Those within the community were bound together through ritual initiation and expulsion rites, through ritual washings and through communal meals. The Essenes also emphasized mysticism and the prophetic tradition of a belief in a Messiah who would come to save the individual soul rather than the Jews as a nation. The discovery of the Dead Sea Scrolls in 1947 has raised the question of the relationship of the Essene community to early Christianity. Although there are crucial differences—for example, Christianity is fundamentally nonexclusive—the Essene emphasis on a close-knit communal relationship, and especially on belief in the Messiah, has a great deal in common with the development of early Christianity.

In contrast to the Essenes, the Zealots, a small but vocal popular minority of political activists, conceived of a Messiah who would bring both religious and political freedom to the Jews as a whole. Since 6 B.C., when the Romans placed the Jews under the joint political control of the non-Jewish Roman administrator, called procurator, and the governor of Syria, the Jews' power over their daily lives was restricted to purely religious affairs. The Zealots felt that the survival of the Jewish way of life would be best ensured by the restoration of control of all areas of Jewish life to the hands of Jewish leaders. Their model for this was the biblical era of Jewish kingship from the line of King David. To that end, the Zealots advocated the kind of resistance to the occupying Romans which had defeated the last non-Jewish holders of the title "King of the Jews," Herod the Great and his son Archelaus, deposed by the Romans in 6 B.C., only after many Jews had lost their lives.

The first Christians comprised a sect within Judaism smaller than those of the Essenes and Zealots. Their emergence can be seen to have three main phases. In the first, around A.D. 28–29, we see Jesus, a Jew from Nazareth, preaching to other Jews first in Galilee and then in Jerusalem. In the second or apostolic stage, after the crucifixion of Jesus around A.D. 30, those Jews who were associated with Jesus and affected by him emerge as a community who assemble in Jerusalem to spread the word of their experiences to other Jews. Before long, this community extended its mission to preach to the Gentiles; in this third stage it established a Gentile mission at Antioch. Fifty years after the crucial crucifixion the community had broken away from its Jewish origins and Christianity became a completely Gentile sect.

The first Christians did not call themselves by that name. They were known among their fellow Jews as "Nazarenes" because their leader, Jesus, grew up in Nazareth. The crucial event for Christianity, of course, is the life and death of this leader whose impact was so powerful that his followers ultimately broke with their ancient Jewish roots. Paradoxically, however, this is the stage in the emergence of Christianity about which we know least. There are few contemporary references to Jesus. Most of the information that we have is legendary rather than historical. It is sifted from the conflicting versions and differing details of the accounts in the Gospels of Matthew, Mark, Luke, and John. These accounts were written from forty to seventy years after the events by men interested in advancing the spread of Christianity. What little we do know about Jesus, however, establishes him as a man familiar with the Jewish Law and tradition, who sought to change that tradition from within. Jesus was a devout Jew whose faith in the central beliefs of Judaism was never in question. He believed in one God who had chosen to reveal His Will to the Jews alone. He respected the centrality of the moral precepts of those Laws which God had handed down. But, like the members of the other sects we have seen, Jesus sought to get at the spirit of that Law and to understand what was necessary for true obedience to God's Laws, and what was superfluous. To this end he criticized some interpretations of the Law by the scribes and Temple priests, and appealed instead to everyday religious experience and to common sense.

Little is known about Jesus' earliest years from the time of his birth sometime between 6 B.C. and A.D. 6 until some time around A.D. 28 when he appeared in public as a forceful preacher and healer in the hills of Galilee near Nazareth. Legends stress his attraction to the personalized mystical preachings of John the Baptist, a religious recluse who espoused a form of ascetic

Judaism very close to that of the Essenes. Concerned with salvation of the individual soul, John the Baptist stressed the impending approach of the heavenly kingdom and urged repentance. In doing so, he continued the tradition of the ancient Judaic prophets, men believed to have special powers to commune with the spirit of God and a mission to spread the word of their direct revelations. Jesus' preachings place him in that tradition as well, although some theologians see an innovation in his emphasis on a heavenly kingdom that was not merely to come but was in fact also already at hand.

Whether his message contained this different emphasis or not, there was clearly a sense of immediacy in Jesus' presentation of his teachings. The people of Galilee were predominantly peasants, fishermen, craftsmen, and farmers. Their ways were generally more simple than the people of a region like Jerusalem, their level of culture and education characteristically lower. Although Jesus preached to the scholars as well as the laymen, his use of parables together with the direct display of his powers of healing seemed especially appealing to the latter. They could readily appreciate his insistence on the intent of the Law rather than formalities of practice as well. After early success on his home ground, Jesus was moved to spread the word to the established seat of power of the Jewish community, the authorities associated with the Temple at Jerusalem. Jesus' ideas were received differently by those leaders who saw themselves in charge of the welfare of the Jewish community as a whole. Probably after less than a year Jesus ran into conflict with the more prominent religious and political authorities.

At issue was the way Jesus invoked his own experience and authority instead of appealing to that of scribal and priestly tradition, and the way he urged others to do so as well. On religious grounds this claim to his unique authority, together with his criticism of the authority of the Temple and scribal tradition, led to the charge of false prophecy and blasphemy. There were political factors as well. Jesus was not a Zealot; like the Essenes, his concern was for individual rather than political salvation. In fact, he preached separation of religion and state. However, the area Jesus came from, Nazareth in Galilee, had long been the seat of Zealot-inspired religious and political revolt, and Jesus could not escape those associations. Galilee had been particularly active in revolts against the last holders of the title "King of the Jews," Herod the Great, his son Archelaus, and their followers.

Within Jesus' generation, in a revolt against the Romans after the death of Herod in 4 B.C., Jewish insurgents in the vicinity of Nazareth were burned and two thousand Zealots crucified. Two years later, Galileans under Judah, son of Hezekiah, led an attack on the Romans that was instrumental in getting Archelaus deposed. Shortly thereafter a people's uprising led by Judah the Galilean protested the census under the new system of Roman procurators. For these reasons the Jewish leaders in Jerusalem feared not only a messianic pretender, but one who might incite political revolution that would bring reprisal on the rest of the Jews. The Roman leaders, on the other hand, feared a political uprising under a pretender to the title of "King of the Jews." The common penalty for those actions under Roman rule was crucifixion. Thus, like the Galilean insurgents before him, Jesus was crucified at Golgotha outside Jerusalem sometime around A.D. 30.

This crucifixion of Jesus the Jew from Nazareth—an event that was barely recorded by contemporary witnesses—had enormous impact on the history of the Western world. In fact, the Church as an institution begins with the reaction to events after Jesus' death. Although Gospel accounts of specific details vary—for example, whether the first to witness Jesus risen from the dead after his burial was Peter (Luke), James (Matthew, John) or Mary Magdelene (Mark and John)—those closest to Jesus experienced him as unconquered by death. They believed that God had resurrected Jesus from the dead, and that by that act God vindicated Jesus as Lord, the Messiah expected according to Jewish prophetic tradition to return to earth to establish the reign of God for all time.

The formation of the Church begins shortly after the resurrection, on the resurrection evening, or on the Jewish feast of Shavuot, or Pentecost, commemorating the revelation of the Law on Mt. Sinai. In both cases the disciples of Christ—twelve men led by Peter, believed chosen by Jesus before his death because of his close association with them during his lifetime—experienced the Holy Spirit (a term associated in Judaism with the tradition of prophecy) directly from Jesus in a unique way. This experience confirmed the Galileans in their faith and inspired them to urge others to believe and repent. Thus, the Catholic Church as we know it today traces its authority from its direct descent from these first believers, or apostles, meaning "those who are sent," as they later became known.

These apostles, who became founders of the Catholic

Church, were pious Jews praised for their devotion to Jewish ritual and custom. At first their mission was to spread the good news, or gospel, and persuade others to acknowledge Jesus as the Messiah. This gospel did not initially require a break with Judaism, the Temple or the Law. On the contrary, the apostles took it for granted that the act of resurrection was continuous with the past revelations of God to his people, an extension of the old covenant between Abraham and God symbolized by circumcision.

The disciples' attempts at conversion began with their fellow-Jews in Jerusalem with good response. They, of course, were not well received by the Sadducees, who rejected the concept of resurrection; but their serious attention to determining the revealed Will of God did attract some Pharisees, while they continued to receive the popular support Jesus' preaching had attracted. Within a decade or two, substantial groups of Jewish Christians in Jerusalem and the surrounding countryside of Judaea had formed.

When the apostles slowly spread the word beyond Jerusalem to the numerous Jewish communities scattered along the Mediterranean coast, they still concentrated on the "lost sheep" of the House of Israel. The first record of opposition to the apostles takes place in the synagogues of the Dispersion, when Stephen, leader of Jews with Roman ties, was arrested, denounced, and stoned to death for speaking against the Temple. His martyrdom also caused the apostles to scatter and thus extend the areas of their preaching. The fact that the leadership of the apostles in Jerusalem soon passed from Peter to James indicates some internal conflict among the Jewish Christians as well. In fact, from that point on, Jerusalem remained the more conservative base of the Jewish wing of Christianity.

Ultimately, Jerusalem became opposed to Antioch, capital of Syria and third city of the Roman Empire. At Antioch, the term "Christian" is used for the first time. There we see the rise of a Gentile mission which led to a break with Judaism. At issue were the requirements for the Gentile converts to Christianity. Many of the Gentile converts were among the so-called "God-fearers," groups of devout Gentiles allowed to become affiliates of synagogues throughout the Dispersion without undergoing circumcision to become a Jew. As the numbers of Gentile converts grew, a conservative faction called Judaizers, undoubtedly fearing to lose the Jewish basis of their sect, demanded that Gentile converts should be required to be circumcised and to obey Jewish Law. The Universalists, on the other hand, felt that Christ's message should not be restricted to Jews but available to all.

Saul of Tarsus, a Cilician Jew and Roman citizen, first came to prominence during this controversy. Originally a student of the famous Pharisee Rabbi Gamaliel and active in the conservative movement in Jerusalem, Saul had a conversion experience that changed the course of Church history. Formerly so ardent a devotee of Mosaic Law he zealously persecuted the disciples, after a direct experience of the risen Jesus on the road to Damascus, he became an equally fervent advocate of the gospel of Christ. Paul, the Roman name by which he was later known, became leader and defender of the Gentiles' right to become Christians without conversion to Judaism. His arguments on their behalf revolutionized the nature of Christianity. Paul saw that the issue was the validity of Mosaic Law. To require circumcision or the practice of Jewish Law meant that faith in the risen Christ was not enough for salvation. Whereas before his conversion Paul was committed to the Judaizers' belief that salvation was attained through adherence to Mosaic Law, now he saw faith in Jesus as enough in itself: ". . . if justification were through the law, then Christ died to no purpose" (Galatians 2:21, RSV). Accordingly, he stressed the gospel as providing liberation from the Law: salvation comes not through "good works," or obeying the Law, but through faith in God's mercy represented in Jesus Christ.

A compromise to this bitter debate was achieved at a council in Jerusalem around A.D. 49, but all issues were not solved for all time. The division between Jerusalem and Antioch arose again in the eleventh-century split between the Eastern and Western Church, while "good works vs. faith" recurred in the sixteenth-century Lutheran reformation.

After this debate, however, Paul emerged as the leader of a vastly changed Church. The Gentiles were required to obey dietary restrictions and to refrain from sexual relations outside marriage, but they were not required to be circumcised. Although Paul still considered himself a practicing orthodox Jew, stripped of its Jewish basis in the Law, the Church was now potentially catholic or universal. From this point on, although records of Jewish Christians remain for several hundred years, their impact on the history of the Church disappears. Increasingly both Jews and Christians denounced Jewish Christians. By A.D. 85, the Nazarenes were formally excluded from Judaism, while Christians came to consider them a deviationist sect at best. On the other hand, the congregations Paul established on his vigorous mission throughout Asia Minor and Greece attest to the growth of Gentile converts.

Christianity and Rome: The Legitimization of the Church

If the task of first-century Christianity was to relate to Judaism, then that of the second century was to deal with the pagan environment. Exactly why these missions had such widespread support will, of course, never be known. Some historians, however, credit at least in part Paul's uncanny ability to adapt to pagan traditions. Important to the pagans were the mystery cults. Each cult was distinctive, so that the Great Mother Cults of the Egyptian Isis and the Anatolian Attis and Cybele had widespread appeal, while the exclusively male, ascetic cult of Mithra, Persian god of light, proved especially popular with the military. All, however, were secret societies whose elaborate initiation rites aimed at union with a divine figure in order to secure liberation, regeneration, and rebirth into eternal life.

By the end of the second century, Paul's de-emphasis on the historical in favor of the divine nature of Jesus made Christianity comparable to these cults. Despite the basic similarity of offering salvation through its divine lord, two crucial differences between Christianity and the other cults point to the continuing importance of Christianity's Judaic heritage. One is morality: while the Gentile cults were amoral at best, for the

Christians, as for the Jews, religion and morality were one. This meant that the Christian who was reborn in Jesus Christ was assured of eternal salvation only by living a life that would give daily proof of this new relationship. Perhaps even more crucial, however, was the Christian belief that their lord Jesus was the one and only Lord. In contrast to this Judaic monotheism, the pagans considered the deities of their cults so non-exclusive that participation in several cults was not incompatible.

This Christian claim to the exclusivity of their God ultimately enabled a clash with the Roman State. The official policy of that state was tolerance of religious pluralism—even incorporating any deities who might seem useful—unless any cult was seen as encouraging harm to the state. The inability of Christians, like the Jews, to recognize gods other than their own set them apart and facilitated suspicion about their being good citizens of the Roman State. In addition to the mystery cults, ancient local gods, the state, and the emperor were often worshiped with religious rites. Judeo-Christian religious principles which prevented complete participation in these rites left Christians especially vulnerable to charges of neglecting the old gods, or "atheism," and encouraging sedition against the state.

In fact, the Christians did not support the Zealot cause of revolt against the Roman State. They were interested in converting the pagans rather than conflict. In contrast to Jewish tolerance for other religions, exhibited by a lack of public denunciation, however, the Christians' zeal for conversion was seen as disregard for pagan Roman tradition and the unity of the state. Thus, the first charges against the Christians are those of disrupting the state. From the Roman officials' point of view, this new cult of Christianity was, after all, led by Jesus, a Jewish criminal executed on such grounds. Paul may have been executed in Rome on the basis of similar charges. Or his execution, like that of Peter, may simply have been part of Nero's first recorded state persecution of Christians in A.D. 64. Both possibilities amount to the same thing, for it is clear that rather than persecuting Christians because of their beliefs, Nero exploited public opinion, which saw Christians as a threat to the order of the state. Nevertheless, Nero's persecution, which was restricted to Rome, did set up a precedent for being put to death because of being Christian.

During the second century being a Christian remained a capital offense in the Roman Empire, but persecution was localized, sporadic, and limited to few in numbers. In fact, publicity provided by such martyrs as Ignatius, Bishop of Antioch, simply spurred the development of Christianity.

It was not until the third century that Christians were persecuted on the basis of their religious beliefs under pressure from increasing barbarian invasions that were easily blamed on the Christians' disrespect for the gods. Severe and serious persecution under Emperor Decius (249–51) required everyone to carry proof of having sacrificed to the gods. But the most sustained and systematic persecution of the Christians was effected by the Emperor Diocletian (284–305) who had established separate rulership of the empire, for the West at Milan and for the East at Nicomedia, as a defense against the barbarians. Persecution of the Christians was most severe in his area, the East, where

Christians representing 10 percent of the population were more numerous. A series of edicts by Diocletian and his co-emperor, Galerius, from A.D. 300-304 purged Christians from the military, leveled the church, and created a bloodbath among the ranks that stopped only in A.D. 311. Then Galerius, near death, abruptly recanted and issued a proclamation of toleration.

Just as the persecutions were renewed, a vision of the risen Christ, this time by a Roman emperor, changed the course of the history of the Catholic Church once more. Constantine, proclaimed sole emperor of the West, attributed his military victory over a rival in A.D. 312 to the help of the Christian God. In A.D. 313 at a meeting with the emperor of the East of Milan, both agreed to a policy of complete religious toleration. Constantine did not formally convert to Christianity until near death in A.D. 337. Although he ultimately favored Christianity, he did not make it the sole official state religion. Nevertheless, his recognition of Christianity did more than end the persecutions. From this point on, Constantine was intimately involved with the development of the Church, while it was increasingly implicated in political decisions. The Church was on the road to alliance with the state.

II

Growth and Consolidation of Structure and Belief

The Growth of Authority

BEFORE WE CAN UNDERSTAND HOW CONSTANTINE'S LEAD-ership altered the organization of the Catholic Church, we need to look at the way that organization had evolved. Most of the consolidation of structure and belief in the early Church took place during the relative respite from external persecution in the second century. But the seeds of the organization of the Church can be seen in the apostolic missions. One of the undoubted attractions for members of the missions Paul established was the sense of belonging to a larger community of believers in the risen Christ. These communities, composed of both Jews and Gentiles from different classes, were bound together in a fellowship through which they attained spiritual union with Christ. Two rituals became especially important. Baptism, at this stage mainly an adult ritual cleansing with water, was required for conversion to Christianity, as it had been for Judaism. But the Christian initiation rite was seen as a way of participating in the death and resurrection of Jesus, a dying to sin and rebirth through the Spirit of Christ.

Similarly, Jesus' command to repeat his last meal with the disciples transformed a communal celebration of fellowship into a sacred ritual, called the Lord's Supper, or Eucharist, from the Greek "thanksgiving." This ritual communion became an important part of the celebration of the resurrection when the Christians met on Sundays, the day of resurrection, rather than on the traditional Judaic Sabbath. Paul called this fellowship or church the mystical body of Christ. Sharing the bread and wine in this communal meal became a way of commemorating Christ's death by participating in his blood and body, and also of celebrating the spirit of his eternal presence. Participation in this meal became so important an expression of membership in the larger community that fragments of the broken bread were often taken to any who were absent through illness or imprisonment. Any serious moral fault would mean temporary or permanent exclusion from the meal. Ultimately, the rite was seen as a re-creation of

Christ's sacrifice, a new covenant replacing that between God and Abraham.

According to Catholic tradition, the Church was organized by Jesus when he appointed the twelve apostles and gave them authority to assume control of the Church after his death. Paul, himself not one of the original twelve, defined the term "apostle" to include those who witnessed the resurrection by personally experiencing the Spirit of the risen Christ, and so received unique authorization from Jesus to establish churches. As leaders of communities, the apostles commanded obedience, but they exercised their authority in fellowship with all the other members of the community. Paul acknowledged that in addition to apostles, prophets and teachers were necessary for the fellowship, as well as healers, helpers, administrators, and speakers in tongues (1 Corinthians 12:28).

Because the apostles were primarily traveling missionaries, they needed to have someone in charge while they were away. Although the evidence is scant, they seem to have set up local boards of elders, called equally bishops or presbyters, and deacons, or helpers, to administer collectively under the apostles' long-distance supervision. During the apostolic age the whole Church was considered a priesthood, without distinguishing between clergy and laity. But we can see the beginnings of such a later distinction in the different functions of the presbyter-bishops and the deacons. The presbyter-bishops were associated with the liturgy, or public worship, as the only ones able to perform the rite of the Eucharist. While the deacons were able to assist at that rite, their duties were mainly nonliturgical: managing property and distributing charity. Women appear in this structure as deaconesses, responsible only for administering charity to women.

The two systems, the apostolic overseers and the local ministry, seemed to coexist for a time. But gradually, as the congregations consolidated, the role of the traveling apostles seems to have diminished in favor of that of the local ministry. The transition between the two stages, however, is not at all clear.

The second century saw the Church working out the problems created by such a transition. By that time several different kinds of Christianity were beginning to emerge. These sects raised questions about belief within the Church. With the generation of apostles and prophets gone, the Church had to face the problem of how to maintain the authority the apostles had established. The Church's solution was an assertion of an unbroken tradition of continuity of authority from the apostles.

We can also see the way questions about belief affected the structure of the Church in the way the Church responded to questions raised by one very popular sect, the Christian Gnostics. The discovery of texts of Gnostic writings at Nag Hammadi in upper Eygpt in 1945 has greatly increased our understanding of the way this sect affected the development of the early Church.

The term "Gnostic," from the Greek *gnosis,* meaning "knowledge," is used to describe several early Christian sects with different and sometimes rival ideas. Basically, however, the sects shared a dualistic view of human nature that emphasized the superiority of spiritual knowledge and understanding over physical matter. Because the Gnostics saw the material world as the creation of inferior or incompetent powers, and therefore alien from God and goodness, they rejected the idea of the human nature of Christ as an illusion at best, and insisted that he was a purely spiritual being. They felt that the way to come to know God was through understanding the self, and they saw Jesus as a guide to opening up this spiritual understanding.

These Gnostic notions about the nature of God and the value of spiritual knowledge came to affect the choice of sacred texts. The Bible for first-century Christians was the Old Testament. By the second century this sacred text was supplemented by oral and written accounts of the life of Jesus, some of which would eventually comprise the New Testament. In addition to such Gospels as those of Mark, Luke, Matthew, and John were rival written accounts such as the Gnostic Gospels, recently rediscovered at Nag Hammadi. The Gnostics claimed these writings were sacred texts containing secret knowledge taught by Jesus to his disciples. The Church, on the other hand, considered them spurious.

In this way, Gnostic beliefs challenged the authority by which texts were considered sacred. This Gnostic challenge established the clear need for both a fixed canon, or authoritative list of common sacred texts, and for an explanation of its principles of selection. The first to establish such a canon and explanation was the Gnostic Marcion. Marcion questioned the authority of both the Old Testament and the four Gospels, and thereby challenged the principle of continuity between the Old Testament and Christ's gospel. He rejected the Old Testament completely, arguing that the God of justice of the Old Testament Jews was vastly inferior to the God and Father of Jesus associated with love. Marcion also rejected three Gospels entirely on the basis of their erroneous assumption of continuity with the Old Testament, and proposed a revised Gospel of Luke with authorship attributed to Paul.

The status of the Old Testament was not in question for the Church fathers, however, and Marcion was excommunicated for his denial of the fundamental Christian belief that Christ's coming was a fulfillment of Old Testament prophecy. Marcion's revisions of the Gospels and the Gnostic claim of the sacred nature of the Gnostic Gospels, however, pointed to the need for a definitive principle of selection of authoritative accounts of the life of Jesus. Led by Irenaeus, bishop of Lyons (185–90), the Church fathers successfully asserted that only those accounts written by the apostles themselves or their close associates should be considered authoritative.

On this basis the Gnostic Gospels were rejected as fraudulent, while most of the letters of Paul and the Gospels of Matthew, Mark, and Luke were accepted as genuine. Later, when their authorship by the apostles was confirmed, the Gospel of John, certain letters of Paul, and other works were also included. By A.D. 390 most of the New Testament as we know it today was finalized, and the principle of the authority of the body of the living Church interacting with the written testimony of the apostles was firmly established.

Gnostic disagreement with the Church positions also helped shape general beliefs into a unifying creed. This official confession of the essential articles of faith required by the Catholic Church was formulated to exclude many Gnostic beliefs. The articles of Irenaeus's "Rule of Faith" asserted the Church's belief in one God, Father and Creator of all things, as opposed to Gnostic dualism. It expressed belief in the incarnation, or embodiment of God in the human form of Jesus, as opposed to the Gnostic denial of Jesus' human status. In addition, it expressed faith in the Holy Spirit as the prophetic inspiration which foretold the coming of Jesus as Christ the Savior. By helping define the Gnostics as deviates from the true faith, or heretics, the creed contributed to their leaving the Church between A.D. 80–150. In fact it established a pattern for orthodoxy against which heretics would be tested for centuries to come.

Finally, Gnostic attacks also helped shape the structure of the administration of the Church. The Gnostics, in effect, denied the necessity of Church leadership to attain salvation by their claim to have secret teachings from Jesus which the Church did not possess, and by their emphasis on self-knowledge. The principle of apostolic succession was also used to thwart the attack on the emerging presbyterian Church structure involved in this Gnostic challenge. The Church fathers countered the Gnostics by emphasizing the authority of the Church leaders. They argued against the Gnostic secret teachings that any important teaching would have been transmitted by the apostles Peter and Paul to the original Church founders, who in turn would have passed them on to the contemporary leaders of the Church, the presbyters or bishops. This meant, in effect, that only these leaders had authorization and direct access to the revelation the apostles witnessed. Thus, Irenaeus of Lyons could present a unified universal Church with a tradition of revelation unbroken by time.

Ultimately the Church emphasis on leadership involved an endorsement of an emerging hierarchy. Clement of Rome censured the overthrow of church elders and their replacement by new clergy at Corinth in A.D. 96. By arguing that because the original elders stood in due succession from the apostles, they should not have been replaced by members at large, Clement in effect endorsed a fixed clergy separated from the laity. In addition, there was an increasing movement within the Church to concentrate the authority of the elders into one senior official, now called the bishop, from the Greek *episkopos*, or "overseer," to distinguish him from the other presbyters, now subordinate to him. The Gnostics, who rotated duties equally among men and women by drawing lots, criticized such separation of functions as unspiritual and worldly. They in turn were criticized for allowing women to perform such functions as teaching, healing, exorcising, and possibly even baptizing. Such defenders of the emerging hierarchy as Ignatius of Antioch (d. 107), the first to use the term "Catholic Church," insisted that the authority of the bishop over the rest of the Church mirrored the authority of the Divine Monarch, whose representative on earth the bishop was.

The Gnostic attacks helped point out the advantage of having a single bishop as the representative of the Church and the focus of unity. By the mid-second century this system, called the monarchical episcopate, was firmly established. The bishop alone had the right to lead public worship and administer sacraments, and especially to ordain his fellow presbyters, He was responsible for communicating with the other churches and for representing his church at general gatherings.

The first meeting, or synod, of bishops to discuss common problems and solutions probably took place in Asia between A.D. 160–75. In time, a gradual hierarchy of churches emerged, often on the basis of political importance. Provincial churches became subordinate to other churches, which acquired metropolitan status. In turn, Rome, Alexandria, and Antioch acquired supra-metropolitan status over the metropolitan churches. Ultimately Rome became distinguished as the unique center of Church unity because of its special status as the official residence or "see," from the Latin *sedes*, of the apostles Peter and Paul, as capital of the Empire, and as willing distributor of its considerable wealth. Special honor and authority then became invested in the bishop of Rome, who became known as the Pope.

The Shape of Belief

The Church that Constantine inherited was ready for the kind of leadership he could provide. By the time he became emperor, the Church had been firmly established not only in Asia Minor and Greece, but throughout North Africa, Gaul, Germany, Spain, and Britain. During the second and third centuries it had developed a well-defined structure and system of belief, and many were beginning to see the destiny of the Church and the state as being providentially intertwined. In the fourth century with Constantine's help the Church became integrated into the everyday life of the citizens of the Roman Empire. Initially, Constantine seemed to see no conflict between Christianity and the predominant Roman sun-worship, which he headed as emperor. The result was an accommodation of the beliefs and practices of paganism and Christianity. In 321 Constantine passed a law making Sunday, a day important to both Christians and pagan sun-worshipers, the official day of rest. He also instituted the celebration of Christ's birthday on December 25, traditionally the feast of the birth of the sun god.

Constantine's fusion of Christian and Roman beliefs and practices also shaped the Church into a Roman institution. Constantine's habit of endowing the Church with buildings and monuments to mark important events established a pattern of church architecture based on Roman meeting halls and palaces. In 324 when he moved the capital of the Empire to Byzantium, renamed Constantinople, Constantine built many churches at his "new Rome," including two great ones dedicated to peace and the holy apostles. He erected several basilicas, such as those over the tombs of Peter at Rome and Christ in Jerusalem. He also gave the bishop of Rome his Lateran palace as residence, which it remained until 1308.

Increasingly, Constantine actively advocated Catholicism. His support of the Church facilitated mass conversions of pagans. The result was the incorporation of many pagan customs into the Catholic liturgy, or system of worship. These customs included devotion to relics, the use of the kiss as a sign of reverence for holy objects, the practice of kneeling, the use of candles and incense, and an increased use of ceremonies patterned on those used in the imperial court.

The increased ritualization of the liturgy, along with the elevated status Constantine gave to the Catholic clergy comparable to that of the pagan priests, helped further the separation between clergy and laity in the Catholic Church. Constantine recognized the clergy as a distinct social class exempt from military service and forced labor. He increased the authority of the bishops by giving civil authority to their judicial decisions. He also enabled the Church to accumulate wealth by legalizing bequests to it.

Earlier the Catholic clergy had not been sharply differentiated from the laity in their lifestyle. They had married, raised children, and supported themselves by secular trades or occupations. As the Church was able to accumulate money, however, the clergy became paid for their clerical services. They increasingly withdrew from their secular occupations until by Constantine's day such withdrawal was obligatory.

Ultimately Constantine associated the needs of the Church with those of the state. In the interests of attaining unity in both, he did not hesitate to intervene in Church affairs. In North Africa, Constantine found disagreement about the validity of sacraments administered by a minister who had turned over the Scriptures to pagan authorities during the persecution by Diocletian. Donatus, bishop of Carthage (d. 355), and his followers refused to recognize the appointment of such a minister whose faith they felt was no longer pure. Constantine referred the matter to a council of bishops at Arles who ruled against Donatus in 314. When the Donatists protested the decision, Constantine, claiming his duty to protect worship, eliminate error, and maintain order, stepped in on his own to enforce the Arles decision. The integration between Church and state can be seen from the assumption, after Arles, that bishops deposed by church councils would be exiled to prevent their stirring up further trouble.

Constantine encountered a more serious dispute in the East at Alexandria in Egypt. There the issue was the exact nature of Christ. On the basis of New Testament accounts, Jesus had become an object of faith worshiped as Lord and Savior with God. As Christ, Jesus was seen as the Divine Son, or *Logos*, meaning Word, whose incarnation, or taking on human form to participate in the crucifixion and resurrection was the means by which the Divine Father ensured the salvation of the world. The question arose of the exact relationship between God the Father and Christ His Son. What aspects of God's nature did Christ share? Was Christ equal with God? Did Christ therefore always exist? Or was Christ merely created by God, and therefore more limited and subordinate? The formulations about the nature of Christ became known as Christology.

In Alexandria the Christological debate became heated. The bishop of Alexandria, representing one school of thought, proclaimed that as *Logos* or Word, Christ's being was divine and had existed from all eternity before coming into the world. Another group, however, led by his presbyter Arius, challenged the bishop. Whereas the Gnostics had denied Christ's humanity, the Arians, as this group was called, denied Christ's divinity. By asserting that as *Logos*, Christ did not have prior existence before the Father created him, the Arians declared Christ more limited than God, and therefore subordinate to Him.

Once again Constantine intervened in Church doctrine in order to maintain unity and peace. At Nicaea in 325 he called a council of bishops, which was the first ecumenical or world council, to settle the dispute. At this meeting, which was attended predominantly by Eastern bishops, Arianism was solidly denounced. A creed associated with the Nicene Council, and still recited in the Catholic Church today, asserts that the Son was begotten and not created, and that he shares in the divine nature fully and equally.

The council did not end the Arian controversy, however. Dissatisfaction arose over the Greek term *homoousios* in the Nicene creed, indicating that the Son was consubstantial or "identical in essence" with the Father. This formulation was defended by the Nicenes, led by Athanasius, bishop of Alexandria, as the only term that would indicate that while Father and Son are separate in identity, they share one divine nature. Many Eastern bishops, however, preferred the formulation *homiousios*, indicating that the Son's essence is *like* the Father's, as a perfect image resembles its original. Theology and politics became intertwined. The issue was bound up with increasing tension between Eastern and Western bishops, and rival factions appealed to successive emperors for support. Eventually Constantine's son Constantius, who became sole ruler in 350, supported a formulation that favored the Arians at a council in Constantinople in 360.

In the meantime, questions about the third person of the Trinity were raised: What was the nature of the Holy Spirit and what was the relationship of the Spirit to the Son and to the Father? Athanasius asserted that the Spirit was also consubstantial with the Father and Son.

While sharing the same essence, however, there was a difference between the Son and the Spirit. This distinction was formulated as "the son is the begotten of the Father," that is, made flesh, while "the Spirit proceeds of the Father," that is, issues as spirit.

After a brief return to paganism under the emperor Julian the Apostate (361–3), the pro-Christian imperial policies instituted by Constantine finally resulted in the merger of the Church and the state. This occurred in 380 when the emperor Theodosius I proclaimed Catholicism the official state religion. The strong hand of the state could be seen in the council he assembled at Constantinople in 381. There Arianism was condemned as heresy, the Nicene creed was reaffirmed, and the doctrine of consubstantiality of the Spirit was endorsed, giving the doctrine of the Trinity its definite form. The strong stand against Arianism was reinforced by further legislation against other heresies several years later. Finally, in 391 the rites and practices of paganism were declared illegal and its priesthood abolished. At the same time exemption from taxes and immunity from civil trials were transferred from pagan priesthood to Catholic clergy, and the pagan practice of the temple as a place of sanctuary was transferred to the Catholic Church.

The councils of Nicaea and Constantinople, however, did not end the Christological controversies. Once the divinity of Christ was established, questions arose about the relationship of Christ's humanity to his divine nature. Once again doctrine was inextricably bound up with politics. The question divided two rival schools of theology in the East: Antioch and Alexandria. Since Nestorius, who represented the Antioch school, was also archbishop of Constantinople, the issue was further complicated. Alexandria was still smarting from the council of Constantinople's elevation of Constantinople to the position previously held by Alexandria as second city to Rome. Nestorius taught a doctrine that seemed to attribute two separate and non-interchangeable natures to Christ, one human and the other divine. The Nestorians, as his followers were called, argued that the Son of God was not born, but rather that Christ was born a man, in whom God dwelt. For this reason, Nestorius claimed that the Virgin Mary was technically not the Mother of God, but the Mother of Christ. The last statement especially was taken as proof that Nestorius denied Christ's divinity, and at a council at Ephesus in 431 Nestorius was condemned as a heretic and exiled.

The Alexandrians, on the other hand, known as the Monophysites, meaning "one nature," believed that the union of human and divine natures of Christ was so strong that it constituted one nature whose aspects were interchangeable. Thus, they felt one could legitimately say that God suffered on the cross, or that Jesus created the world. Partly in reaction to the Nestorians, however, they tended to overemphasize Christ's divinity to the exclusion of his humanity and insist that his one nature was divine.

The Council of Chalcedon in 451 achieved some resolution to these issues by taking a middle path between the Nestorian and Monophysite positions. The council's formulation declared that the difference between the divine and human natures is preserved, yet both are united in one person and substance in Christ. The result of this formulation was an increasing emphasis in the Catholic liturgy on the gulf between the human and the divine.

The intricacies of the Christological controversy were developed primarily by the Greek-speaking bishops of the older Eastern Church. In the Western Roman Church, however, by the third century Latin became the preferred language over Greek. A by-product of the Arian controversy was its stimulation of further theological speculation by the Latin-speaking Western Church.

The African Catholic Church looked to Latin Rome for guidance rather than to the Greek East. In fact, its missionaries were probably the first to translate the Bible into Latin. By the fifth century the Latin Bible was so established as the Authoritative Version that Jerome's Revised Version aroused deep opposition. Contemporary with Jerome, Latin Africa saw the rise of a bishop named Augustine whose contribution to Latin theology in the West made his influence on the Catholic Church second only to that of Paul.

Like Paul, Augustine became a convert to Christianity in his adult life. Unlike Paul, however, Augustine (b. 354) was raised in a Christian home. His father was a pagan who converted to Christianity late in life, while his mother, Monica, who profoundly influenced him, was a devout Christian, who had Augustine baptized and given Christian instruction as a child. Nevertheless, Augustine's conversion was a long and deliberate process.

Augustine's famous *Confessions* reveal the progress of his rejection of the life of sensual and material gratification which had absorbed him since adolescence. He lived with a concubine for fifteen years while pursuing an extensive education in Latin literature and rhetoric, leading to posts as professor of rhetoric in Carthage and Rome.

The birth of his illegitimate son in 372, together with reading Cicero's *Hortensius*, inspired Augustine to search for essential truths in the Christianity he had abandoned. However, he was repulsed by the crude style of the Scriptures in comparison to the Latin classics, and felt the same discrepancy between the God of the Old Testament and the New as the Gnostic Marcionites. Instead, he was attracted to Manichaeism, a popular religious sect that also rejected the Old Testament, and was characterized by a radical dualism. The Manichees saw the world as a mixture of good and evil, associated with light and dark. They saw human life as a struggle for freedom from the dark Satanic matter of which humans are composed. To this end they felt that God gave humanity a portion of light which could lead to salvation through self-knowledge. The prophets of this salvation included Buddha, Zoroaster, Jesus, and Mani, a Babylonian who lived between 216–17.

Sex was seen as a hindrance to salvation, and women as seducers who would prevent it. The Elect or perfect followers of Mani, who were considered predestined to salvation, renounced sexuality and the material world. A lesser order, called Hearers, were allowed to marry, but encouraged to hope for reincarnation as an Elect by living according to simple moral rules. Augustine lived as an ardent Hearer for nine years, converting many of his friends as well.

By the time Augustine was appointed professor of rhetoric at the court of the Emperor in Milan in 384, he was already disillusioned by the oversimplification in the Manichaean answers. At Milan he was impressed by the intellectual presentation of the Catholic faith by Ambrose, bishop of Milan. At the same time Augustine was influenced by the profound sense of the spiritual unity of all things in Neoplatonic philosophy, and by the account of the incarnation of Christ in the letters of Paul. Augustine's attraction to what he felt were the irreconcilably opposed spiritual and material worlds was resolved only after deep internal struggle. Finally, inspired by a child's voice directing him to read St. Paul, he abandoned his plans for furthering his worldly career through marriage. After retiring to a country villa for contemplation, he was converted and baptized by Bishop Ambrose at Easter in 387.

His mother died shortly thereafter, and Augustine barely had returned to Africa and established a small ascetic community at Thagaste when his son also died. In 391, while on a casual visit to Hippo, Augustine was reluctantly persuaded to be ordained as presbyter. He moved his community to Hippo, where he was ordained bishop in 395, and remained till his death in 430.

Augustine was an enormously industrious leader of the African Church, acting as episcopal judge, administering property, counseling his priests, and taking part in the great councils. He wrote thirty-three books between 395–410, and his sensitivity to his audience made his many sermons and lectures immensely popular. An excellent speaker, he identified with his hearers and gave life to abstract thought by examples of his own struggles in leading a virtuous life.

Much of Augustine's energy was spent refining Catholic doctrine against the positions of heretics. At

Hippo he was immediately faced with the schism between the Donatists and the Catholics, dating back to the time of Constantine. At first Augustine arranged meetings to try to reconcile the two groups. Beyond disagreements about whether validity lay in the sacraments themselves or in the priest who administered them, however, the Donatists and Catholics held two fundamentally opposed views about the nature of the Church. Isolated from the churches of Jerusalem and Rome, the Donatists claimed to be the church of true African Christianity as it existed before Constantine. As such, it was a pure and exclusive community undefiled by contact with an impure world. The Catholics, on the other hand, felt that a church should not be so sharply separated from the world, but rather should embrace all of humanity, both sinners and saints. The Catholics also stressed their participation with the overseas churches in a truly universal Church.

When it was clear that no agreement would be found, Augustine, reluctantly at first, endorsed the current policy of the Roman Empire in using coercion to repress heresy. In 412 an imperial edict ordered the dissolution of the Donatist Church. Much later Augustine's treatise justifying the state's right to suppress non-Catholics in the interests of their spiritual development proved highly influential as a rationale for the medieval Inquisition.

Augustine's justification of the enforced conversion of the Donatists was based on a view of human nature that was attacked as Manichaean pessimism by Pelagius, a visiting British monk renowned as a speaker on spiritual and moral matters. Augustine believed in the hereditary transmission of original sin through the sexual act. He felt that as a result of Adam's fall, human nature was so corrupt and naturally inclined toward evil that humanity lost the capacity to choose to do good, except by God's grace. Pelagius, on the other hand, was concerned with the human responsibility for sin, which depends on free choices of the will confronted by the possibility of right and wrong. He rejected the concept of hereditary original sin passed down through the reproductive process. Rather, he stated that humanity has a natural ability to reject evil and seek good and therefore sin is voluntary imitation of Adam's disobedience.

Pelagius's views implied that God's grace was not the necessary first step towards virtuous action. Augustine accused him of denying the human need for grace. In fact this was not true. Pelagius acknowledged an unmerited gift of grace in the forgiveness of sins, and spoke of grace as a divine aid conveyed through such moral exhortations as the Commandments and the supreme example of Christ. But Augustine attacked the notions of teaching and example as an external view of grace that was contrary to the internal grace of the love of God poured into our hearts by the Holy Spirit according to St. Paul.

Augustine also felt that Pelagius's rejection of original sin denied the necessity of infant baptism. Again, Pelagius agreed that unbaptized babies would not be admitted into heaven, but felt that surely, by God's mercy, they and virtuous pagans, would at least be sent to a third place, or limbo, rather than hell. To this, Augustine violently objected. His doctrine of predestination maintained that because of original sin, all humanity, by justice, deserves to be condemned to hell. The miracle is that by God's mysterious mercy a few are predestined to be saved.

Augustine succeeded in having the African bishops condemn the main teachings of Pelagius as dangerous heresy in 416. In 418 an imperial edict banished Pelagians from Rome as a threat to peace, perhaps spurred by a Pelagian socialist tract castigating the rich for irresponsibility toward the poor and for maintaining power by torture and cruelty.

The Pelagian controversy was extremely important for the way it resulted in formulating basic theological doctrines about original sin, free will, and grace. Augustine emerged with an international reputation for his elaboration of these doctrines. Only his concept of predestination was rejected. His defense of the concept of grace won him the title "Doctor of Grace." As a result of the controversy, infant baptism became instituted. His other articulations were accepted as the orthodox positions of the Catholic Church, as was his statement on the Trinity, designed to eliminate every possibility of Arian subordination by declaring that the Spirit proceeds not just from the Father, but from the Father and the Son. This addition, known as the "filioque," was quickly accepted in the West, but became disputed in the seventh and eighth centuries by the Eastern Church.

Augustine's association of original sin and sexuality did a great deal to reinforce the growing tendency of the Church to consider that the sexual impulse can never be free of some element of lust, and to justify sex and marriage only by the intention to have children. Virginity and celibacy had always been seen as laudable ideals, and the example Augustine set for other bishops by his own ascetic way of life was extremely influential. During Augustine's time many bishops were married and wealthy. Augustine, however, required his priests to live with him and take vows of poverty, celibacy, and obedience to a strict rule. Many of these priests later spread these ideals throughout the African Church, and so encouraged the growing tendency to feel that celibacy should be required of bishops on the grounds that sexual intercourse was incompatible with the sacred character of the clerical state. Augustine's model not only encouraged the growing practice of establishing monastic communities that would begin to flourish in the middle ages. By transforming a predominantly asocial lay movement into an organization of priests with vows adapted to the sacraments of the Church, he incorporated monasticism into the Church.

Pelagius had visited Africa to seek refuge from the sack of Rome by the Goths in 410, a catastrophe which aroused widespread emotion and fear throughout the Roman Empire. Many pagans attributed this disaster to the empire's abandonment of the old gods for Christianity. In response, Augustine wrote the massive *City of God*, which criticized pagan religion and justified Christianity. In the course of that work Augustine outlined a concept of Christian history which became an important part of the doctrine of the Catholic Church. Through biblical revelation history is seen as a continuing struggle between two cities, the Earthly City and the City of God. The Earthly City is made up of those who are filled with self-love and pursue only earthly goods. Even Christian Rome is part of this empire and will pass away as all empires have. Humanity's goal, however, lies beyond this transitory life in the

City of God which lasts eternally. The City of God embraces all those who commit themselves to the spiritual values of God. The true meaning of history does not lie in the flux of external events, but in the internal drama of sin and redemption.

Unlike Constantine, Augustine did not see the interests of the Roman Empire and the kingdom of God as entirely identical. To him the line between the Earthly City and the City of God was not simple and clear because it had to do with commitment to internal values. The state was not simply the Earthly City of self-love, nor was the Church completely identical with the City of God. There were enemies within and without. For these reasons Augustine developed the concept of the just war and declared that the Church must militantly seek out and convert those who stray through ignorance or error. This formulation had important consequences for the relationship between the Church and the barbarians after the fall of the Roman Empire.

Augustine lived to see that collapse. The Vandals attacked Africa in 429. Before Augustine died a year later, however, he had laid firm foundations for the medieval Catholic Church.

III

The Medieval Achievement

The Rise of the Papacy

AT THE COLLAPSE OF THE ROMAN EMPIRE THE CHURCH provided valuable leadership. By the end of the fourth century the Church had become responsible for much of the social as well as the spiritual welfare of its members. Especially in the cities, many churches, as wealthy landowners, were responsible for maintaining the poor, the aged, and the oppressed. Prayer to saints who would intercede in spiritual matters, popular from the third century on, was a natural transfer to the spiritual realm of the social situation on earth. Elected by

51

both the clergy and the people, the bishops became popular authorities expected to help the people through such everyday matters as obtaining better jobs and steering through the bureaucracies of the courts.

The state gave increasing legal authority for social welfare to the bishops. Ultimately their prestige and sphere of influence was even felt by secular authorities. In 390, Augustine's esteemed Bishop Ambrose had the power to make the Emperor Theodosius perform public penance at the door of the Cathedral in Milan to atone for the gratuitous massacre of the citizens of Thessalonica. In the confusion of the barbarian attacks, Church leaders were also recognized as authorities capable of negotiating with the barbarian invaders. In 452, Pope Leo I (440–61) traveled to Mantua to meet Attila the Hun and dissuaded him from attacking Rome. In 455, again it was Leo who met the Vandals at the gates of Rome and prevented massacre by limiting the Vandals to a peaceful sack of the city.

Pope Leo exerted an equally strong sense of leadership within the church. Here he was especially forceful in asserting his strong sense of the special status of the bishop of Rome. Like Pope Damasus before him, Pope Leo emphasized Peter as "the Rock" on which Christ built the Church, and stressed the popes or bishops of Rome, the city where Peter died and was buried, as the rightful successors to Peter's leadership of the Church. In fact, Pope Leo felt that Peter himself spoke through the Popes, who were simply Peters' temporal and mystical representatives. This meant that the Popes' decrees should be received with authority above that of the other patriarchs, as the bishops of Alexandria, Antioch, Jerusalem, and Constantinople were beginning to be called.

The basis of authority within the Church had been the system of episcopal councils which ruled on matters of doctrine and discipline. However, disputes during the Arian and successive controversies pointed to deficiencies in the system. Rivalry for leadership weakened respect for conciliar decisions, as did the Constantine legacy of appealing to emperors, and so allowing political interference in doctrinal decisions.

The Arian disputes also pointed to a clear need for central control. Western Catholicism was mainly Mediterranean, strong in Italy, North Africa, Spain, and the Rhone valley, with some converts in Gaul, Britain, and Ireland. There, the bishop of Rome arose as a natural leader whose importance overshadowed the councils. As the only apostolic see, Rome had an unrivaled status and became a natural court of appeal. In letters called *decretals*, the Popes began to initiate advice to the churches beyond what had been sought. This papal advice began to be collected and consolidated along with the conciliar decisions. Since the doctrinal debates had occurred in the Eastern councils, heretical opinions were also associated with the East. The result was a much better papal record of never having been wrong.

The Eastern Church held the Balkans, Asia Minor, Egypt, Palestine, Syria, and Mesopotamia. There no single patriarchate had the status of Rome, and the conciliar system was much more firmly established. Nevertheless, during the Arian disputes when Rome attempted to act as a court of appeals for Eastern decisions, Eastern patriarchs protested interference in their jurisdiction. Thus, the Council of Chalcedon in 451 saw a move to install Constantinople, as New Rome, as a court of appeal for the East.

At that council Pope Leo acted to further the concept of the primacy of Rome. He wanted the Tome on Christ's nature he wrote and sent accepted without discussion as the word of Peter spoken through papal decree. The Council did accept the Tome, but after deliberation rather than automatically. Leo also successfully squashed the move to elevate Constantinople as equal to Rome, arguing that the grounds of its being an imperial city were secular rather than religious. But he effected a postponement rather than an end to rivalry between the two Romes. Neither the Nestorians nor the Monophysites acquiesced to the Chalcedon decision. In 482 the Emperor Zeno, assisted by the patriarch of Constantinople, issued an edict for reunion. The Roman Pope subsequently excommunicated both men for interfering with Church doctrine without consulting Rome or the episcopal council. The result was a schism between Rome and Constantinople that lasted for thirty-four years.

The Chalcedon rivalry was revived in the seventh-century Monothelete controversy, the last Christological dispute. The patriarch of Constantinople asserted the doctrine of one will of Christ in opposition to the spirit of Chalcedon and the Roman position of Christ's two wills. The resulting twenty-eight year schism between Constantinople and Rome ended in 681 when the emperor replaced the patriarch of Constantinople with one willing to accept the papal position.

The shift of the capital of the Roman Empire to Constantinople greatly enhanced the rise of papal power. While at Constantinople the presence of a Christian emperor eclipsed the power of the patriarch of the Church, the absence of an imperial power at Rome left the bishop of Rome as the most prestigious municipal official. One reason for the shift was the protection of the eastern frontiers from the barbarian invaders.

In the West, as we have seen, the Church was left to deal with the invading Germanic tribes: the Visigoths in Gaul; the Vandals in North Africa; the Franks, Burgundians, and Alemmani along the Western Rhine and north-central Gaul; and the Lombards in Italy. As Arian converts, the Goths and Vandals severely persecuted the Catholics they conquered. Ultimately the Catholics found a champion in Clovis, a heathen ruler of the Franks married to a Catholic princess. Like Constantine, Clovis converted to Catholicism himself after victory in battle in 496. His subsequent conquest of most of Gaul was the result of both his military skill and the cooperation of the Catholic bishops who opened the gates of their cities to him. Clovis's union of the Franks and Catholics into one faith and one kingdom paved the way for the papal foundations of medieval Christianity.

Those papal foundations were firmly forged by Pope Gregory the Great (590–604). Like Pope Leo before him, during the lack of imperial leadership under the Lombards' attacks on Italy, Pope Gregory negotiated with the attackers, saving Rome from being sacked and ultimately bringing about a general peace. In effect he became ruler of central Italy and prepared the way for papal control of the papal states.

Within the Church, like Leo, Gregory also fostered papal primacy. He acknowledged the rights of the patriarchs of the East, but objected that the title "ecumenical bishop," which was being used by the patriarchs of Constantinople, implied "universal bishop" and belonged to the bishop of Rome alone. He also furthered papal primacy by his tight administration within the Western Church. A tireless correspondent, Gregory was in constant contact with church officials. His guidance about doctrine and discipline can be seen in his famous work *Pastoral Care.*

Like Augustine before him, Pope Gregory had abandoned his family wealth and prestigious secular career to embrace a monastic way of life. He ensured that his own wealth and that of the Church were used for public welfare and was an ardent champion of the poor and the peasants. By the sixth century two kinds of monasticism had evolved in the Western Church. At first Celtic monasticism, an austere and individualistic withdrawal from secular life, was dominant. Ultimately the more temperate Rule associated with Benedict, founder of a monastery at Monte Cassino around 520, prevailed. That Rule emphasized a simple communal life, filled with hard work, silence, devotional reading, and obedience to the abbot, or father, of the monastic family. Work came to include physical labor and copying the Bible and even secular classics.

Gregory was concerned to integrate the barbarian conquerors through conversion, and stressed incorporating barbarian customs into Catholic tradition. The monastic system was an important force in these conversions. The fall of the Roman Empire had entailed a collapse of urbanization, and Gregory's goal of bringing religion to ordinary people was facilitated by monastic rural organization. Moreover, the monasteries were permanent self-governing units immediately subject to the Pope. Thus, the Benedictine monks sent by Gregory to convert Britain, and in turn the British monks who converted emerging Germany, tightened papal primacy by being guided directly by Rome. In the seventh century these monasteries, like the Celtic monasteries a century earlier, became important centers for the transmission of Christian culture. In this way Gregory's efforts helped shape a unity of faith and culture that created a new Christendom out of Catholicism and emerging Europe.

In the eighth century the monastic system helped forge the political alliance between the papacy and Franks, which ensured the creation of the new Christendom and the rise of papal power. Such Benedictine monks as Winfrid, later called St. Boniface (675–754), were the chief agents of the Pope in Church reform. Boniface's reform of the Frankish Church, at the request of the king of the Franks, cemented strong ties between the Franks and Rome.

The monks' part in the iconoclastic controversy (726–842) in the Eastern Church helped create the climate that led the papacy to take advantage of those ties. The imperial policy of prohibiting the use of images of Christ and the saints in the Church involved an association of images with superstition and pagan worship present since the earliest days of the Church. It was also in part a convenient attack on the monks. The emperors, plagued by Arab attacks, resented the monks for being a drain on manpower and for their exemption from taxation. The monks not only supported the use of icons as legitimate devotion, but received substantial financial support from the fact that the icons were predominantly located in their monasteries. The alliance of these monks with the papacy against the imperial policy led Pope Gregory II (715–31) to threaten in 729 to look to the newly converted West for support.

The threat became a reality some twenty years later when the emperor's refusal to send military aid against impending Lombard attacks on Rome in 753 caused Pope Stephen II (752–7) to appeal to Pepin, leader of the Franks, for help instead. In addition to the monastic ties with the papacy forged by Church reform, Pepin had recently asked for and received papal sanction for the rulership he had seized from the descendants of Clovis.

Thus, in 754 when Pope Stephen and Pepin met, the king symbolically acknowledged the Pope's authority by prostrating himself before the mounted Pope, and leading the Pope's horse by the bridle. Pepin went beyond symbolic gesture, however. In an agreement called the Donation of Pepin, the Frankish king legitimized the *de facto* rule of the popes, establishing independent papal rule over large portions of Italy. This act authorized the foundation of a papal state that would last until 1870. In return the Pope reannointed Pepin and his two sons, giving them the title "Patricians," or protectors of the Romans, and so installing the Carolingians as leaders of Western Christendom.

This leadership was taken very seriously by Pepin's son Charles, who conquered the Lombards to become their king as well, shortly after becoming sole ruler of the Franks in 771. He confirmed the Pope's rulership of the papal states in 773. However, as most powerful ruler in Italy, Charlemagne, as he became known, was in fact a benevolent patron of the Church. As defender of the faith, he felt free to intervene in the administration of the Church to maintain both order and orthodoxy. The use of one language, Latin, throughout his diverse realm helped forge a common culture. In addition, Charlemagne fostered a common intellectual and moral development through his expansion of the palace schools and the cathedral schools he ordered every bishop to set up. As champion of Christianity, Charlemagne sought to bring heathens under his own authority and that of the Church. By 800 he had virtually reconstituted the social, political, and religious unity of the Western Roman Empire in a territory stretching beyond the Tiber, and bounded by the Ebro, the Elbe, and the North Sea. Continuity with the Roman Empire and the power of the Pope as agent of God were both affirmed at Christmas mass in St. Peter's the same year, when Pope Leo suddenly proclaimed a rather reluctant Charles to be Emperor of the Romans. And so through the union of the Franks, the popes, and the monks the Holy Roman Empire was born.

The union of the Franks and the popes had given the Frankish kings divine sanction and granted the papacy increased temporal power. Charlemagne's supremacy had maintained spiritual and temporal authority in balance. After his death, however, the issue of rivalry for supreme authority in temporal and spiritual matters, latent since Constantine's alliance of Church and state, arose. Since Pope Gelasius (492–6) papal theory had decreed that while the Church was to defer to the emperor in secular matters, the emperor was to defer to the Church and especially to the Pope, as agent of God, in the spiritual realm. In the ninth century successive popes asserted the supremacy of spiritual over temporal power, maintaining the right to interfere in secular matters not only to the crown, but to choose emperors. The collapse of the Holy Roman Empire, however, had a different basis of social organization from that of the Romans. Authority tended to be centered in the leaders of those Germanic tribes who had a direct system of allegiance which took priority over papal direction. If a leader built a church, it was considered his private property and he was free to appoint its staff and control its revenue. In his vast reorganization of the Church, Charlemagne appointed many bishops himself without papal consultation under this policy. The bishops became prized civil servants because of their superior education and administrative skills.

Otto the Great (912–73) then set about restoring the Empire, but with a difference. He sought and received the crown from Pope John XII at St. Peter's in 962. In return he guaranteed the independence of the papal states by confirming the donations of Pepin and Charlemagne. But far from acknowledging papal supremacy, within a year Otto had Pope John deposed and a layman elected in his place. In addition, he declared that before being consecrated, future popes would first have to swear allegiance to the emperor.

Successive monarchs after Otto the Great continued this system of secular appointments to the Church, not only in Germany, but throughout Europe. In the emerging political, social, and economic feudal order, lay appointments were a useful means for kings and their nobles to maintain power. Under the Germanic system, power was attained through control of property, which was passed on through inheritance. The bishops' lack of children ensured that at the bishops' death, land and revenues would be returned to the king. In addition, the kings' control of reappointment allowed them to consolidate power by advancing their own men and curbing the growth of rivals.

Lay control of the Church was symbolized by the feudal ceremony of lay investiture in which the future bishop knelt before the king and swore an oath of submission and allegiance. In exchange he received the king's staff and ring as symbols of being granted spiritual office and temporal jurisdiction over the land. Since the sixth century, country churches were headed by parish priests, called secular clergy, subordinate to the bishops. These too became appointed by the noblemen who owned the land, rather than the Church.

These lay appointments violated the Church law and tradition of the clergy and people electing the bishops. In addition, many abuses arose. It became customary for bishops to pay a substantial fee for their promotion, and soon simony, or buying and selling spiritual benefits for temporal considerations, was pervasive. The clergy were also often untrained and hastily ordained. This haste prevented the old practice of an early marriage which was given up at ordination. As a result, many clergy were marrying or living with women even after becoming ordained.

Ironically, ultimately lay control of the Church revived the flagging spirituality of the Church. Like Charlemagne, such rulers as Henry III (1039–56) were genuinely concerned with the Church as a spiritual and moral guide, and took care to appoint and maintain truly virtuous bishops and popes. These pious men began to reassert the idea of the Church as the body of Christ, entrusted to his apostles whose successors the bishops were. A reform at the monastery of Cluny, established in 910 in Burgundy, allowed the monks to elect their own leader without interference from the nobleman who owned the land. Undoubtedly influenced by this reform, the churchmen attacked the system of lay appointments and investiture. They argued for a return to election of bishops by the clergy and people, and for replacement of lay investiture by examination and ordination conducted by the Church.

This mood for reform led to a revival of Pope Gelasius's theory of the supremacy of the Church over even the Emperor. In 1059 Pope Nicholas II declared that only cardinals, bishops appointed by the Pope as his advisors, were to elect the Pope, although the emperor could confirm the election. But the supreme advocate for papal primacy came with the election of Hildebrand as Pope Gregory VII in 1073. Considered the greatest pope since Gregory I, Gregory VII (1073–85) put reform theory into practice. He instituted the "Gregorian reforms" by issuing decrees against clerical marriage, which declared offspring of the clergy illegitimate; decrees against simony, which denied spiritual powers to immoral clergy; and decrees against lay investiture. In 1075 Gregory also issued a famous statement of unqualified papal authority called the *Dictatus papae*.

This document was based in part on an influential partly-forged history of the papacy called the Pseudo-Isidorian Decretals, produced by the Frankish court around 850. The False Decretals, as they were also called, depicted the Popes as having supreme power, from the earliest times of the Church, to issue laws, validate council decisions, and depose bishops. To the idea of supreme lawgivers within the Church, Pope Gregory added the notion of the Pope as supreme judge on earth. As vicar, or representative of St. Peter and Christ, the Pope had the power to judge right and wrong, and was to be obeyed by all, including emperors, whose disobedience would be met by being excommunicated and deposed. At the same time the Pope could be judged by God alone. In effect, the Pope had become a divine monarch.

Pope Gregory's views led to an inevitable clash between spiritual and secular authorities. The test came when Henry IV defied the decree against appointing his own bishops, declaring Gregory no pope but a false monk. Pope Gregory reacted by excommunicating and deposing the emperor. The result was in effect civil war. Henry traveled to Gregory at Canossa and dramatically stood barefoot in the snow for three days begging for absolution until Gregory gave in. Henry's motives were entirely political, however, and once he regained power, his refusal to yield to Gregory's authority led to his being excommunicated and deposed again. The result was a stand-off, however. Henry in turn deposed Gregory and installed an anti-pope. Gregory died with the populace turned against him when Rome was destroyed by the Normans who came to his aid.

The question of lay investiture was not settled for fifty years. Different compromises were effected in different parts of Europe. In general, the clergy were to elect the bishops. The secular rulers could no longer invest the bishops with the spiritual symbols of their office, the ring and staff. They could invest them with the symbols of their temporal authority, however, and receive homage in return. But the idea of the Pope as a world power was to gain great strides.

The Pope's rise to world power was facilitated by the situation in the Eastern Church. There, the idea of papal primacy in spiritual matters was not questioned, but since the Council of Chalcedon, as we have seen, there was an increasing move for jurisdictional authority for Constantinople in the East. In the seventh century, the Moslem capture of the patriarchates of Alexandria, Antioch, and Jerusalem left Constantinople the unrivaled head of the Eastern Church. The eighth-century iconoclast controversy weakened the Eastern Church when the monks were willing to recognize both the primacy and jurisdiction of the Roman Church in their struggle against imperial interference. At the same time the alliance of the patriarchs of Constantinople with the emperors, together with the fateful alliance between the Franks and Rome, intensified the gap within the Church between Constantinople and Rome.

The iconoclast alliance between the Greek patriarchs and the emperors also involved the Greek preference for abstract art for its emphasis on the divine nature of Christ over the human. This preference reveals the emergence of a self-awareness in the Greek Church of its differences in sensibility from the predominant Latin traditions. Momentary accord was reached in the agreement of Nicaea in 787, reaffirmed in 842, that the images were to be accorded reverence but not worship. But the sense of Greek self-consciousness can also be seen in the ninth-century Photian schism between Constantinople and Rome between 867–79. The main issue was Pope Nicholas I's refusal to recognize the emperor's replacement of the patriarch of Constantinople, Ignatius, by Photius, without consulting Rome. When this irregularity was repaired, the issue became Photius's refusal to acknowledge Rome's primacy. In the course of the struggle, however, Photius, who was the most brilliant lay scholar of his day, came to champion the Greek customs of clerical marriage and Lenten fast ridiculed by the Western emissaries, and to criticize the Western addition of the Augustinian "filioque" to the Creed. In the end, however, peace was made and Photius did acknowledge the supremacy of Rome.

The Eastern resistance to the "filioque" came from the Greek emphasis on the omnipresent and pervasive nature of the Holy Spirit which made the Greeks feel the Spirit descended *through* the Son, *rather than from* the Son. The "filioque" was finally adopted as official doctrine by Rome about 1000. By then, the issue also involved Eastern resistance to the authority of even the Pope to change a formulation which had been decided by an episcopal council.

Disagreement over the "filioque" did not lead to schism, but ultimately the accumulation of doctrinal disputes, growing Greek self-consciousness, and politics in the eleventh century intertwined to create a breach between Constantinople and Rome which remains unhealed to this day. The spark for a series of schisms was rivalry between Constantinople and Rome for jurisdiction over churches in southern Italy recently conquered by the Latin Catholic Normans. When the Pope ordered these churches to switch from using Greek rites to Latin, the patriarch of Constantinople,

Michael Cerulerius, retaliated by ordering Latin churches in Constantinople to adopt Greek rites. In 1053 when they refused, he ordered the churches closed and wrote a letter condemning Latin customs, enraging the Pope.

In 1054 the emperor's and patriarch's attempts at conciliation went so awry that a heated exchange of criticism of Greek and Latin customs led the papal delegation to excommunicate both. Urged on by an outraged populace, the emperor burned the papal order, or bull, of excommunication, while a synod condemned the actions of the delegates, enacting a schism.

Subsequent popes continued to support the excommunication as justified by the patriarch's disobedience and lack of repentance. Subsequent patriarchs refused to seek absolution, and so were regarded as participating in the schism as well. Eventually the whole patriarchate was excommunicated on the basis of continuing to elect and support schismatic bishops.

Pope Urban II's (1088–99) attempts at reconciliation restored good relationships between the sees. His call to the knights of Christendom to crusade against the Moslems in 1095 was motivated in part by his desire to dissipate ill feelings by helping the beleaguered Eastern Christians and so gain their acknowledgment of the Pope as a leader of all Christendom. Unfortunately, however, far from healing the schism between East and West, the Crusades finalized the estrangement. In 1098 the Crusaders seized Antioch and drove the Greek patriarch into exile, installing a Latin patriarch in his place. This act alienated the other Eastern patriarchates, who until this time might have acknowledged Rome over Constantinople. The final blow came in

1203 when the crusaders participated in a sack of Constantinople that wiped out even the churches.

Attempts at reconciliation made at the Council of Lyons in 1276 and at Florence in 1439 remained nominal. The most recent attempts to heal the schism have taken place at the Second Vatican Council in our own time.

The Western knights' enthusiastic participation in the crusades, however, did in fact demonstrate what a world power the Pope had become. By the end of the eleventh century Christendom had expanded to include Denmark, Norway, and Sweden, Bohemia, Poland, Hungary, and Russia, with only the latter following Constantinople into schism. The imperial dress the Pope now wore, including a helmet-shaped headdress surrounded by a crown, or tiara, originally worn by the deified Persian rulers, symbolized the spiritual and temporal authority the papacy now attained.

Pope Leo IX (1048–54) revitalized the papal Curia, or court, by attracting men of energy and vision, who increasingly became statesmen. These men and their successors reorganized and expanded the machinery of papal administration to accommodate their enlarged authority. One of their greatest tools was the revival of general councils. These had formerly been held in the East and were attended mainly by Greek bishops. Now the papacy summoned and presided over predominantly Latin general councils in the West. These councils, together with increased papal decrees, letters, and delegations to churches throughout Christendom dramatized the extent of papal authority and jurisdiction.

Probably the greatest aid to centralization of papal authority, however, came from the papal courts. The great popes of this period were all trained in law, and the comprehensive system of law the papacy developed gave order to a society in which the old systems of law and government had broken down. Here clerks found protection from the often harsher justice of the secular courts, and priests found a guaranteed income with property exempt from secular taxation as well. Religious orders found aid against tyrannical bishops, and bishops found relief from overzealous rulers. In return, rulers benefited from the reasonable discipline and order the papal courts gave to every aspect of the lives of both clergy and laymen. Ultimately this medieval order laid the foundations for modern society as well.

The famous twelfth-century quarrel between Thomas á Becket, archbishop of Canterbury, and his English king, Henry II, was in fact an attempt to increase royal control of the English clergy by decreasing the authority of the papal courts. At issue was Henry's desire to participate in church court decisions, and especially to have clergy found guilty of crimes in papal courts judged by the secular courts as well. The power of the papacy is seen not only in the way Becket's support from the Pope on this issue gave him the power to censure the king, but also in the way popular outrage at Becket's murder in 1170 led Henry himself to do penance at Becket's shrine.

A few years later, in 1176, the same great lawyer-Pope Alexander III (1159–81) won a similar triumph through war. With the help of the major European powers, he defeated the great Emperor Frederick Barbarossa at the Battle of Legnano. When the emperor and pope met in Venice shortly after, Frederick threw off his imperial mantle and knelt before the Pope.

But the zenith of the papal monarchy came with the reign of Pope Innocent III (1198–1216). The concept of papal sovereignty reached its height with Innocent's emphasis on the Pope as entrusted to rule not just the Church, but the world, as vicar of Christ. His intervention in political affairs demonstrated the way temporal power itself derived from the Pope, making him one of the most powerful rulers in history. Seeing a threat to the papal states by being surrounded by Hohenstaufen claims to Germany and north Italy as well as Sicily and south Italy, Innocent steered a precarious course. He gave financial and military support to the rival for the imperial throne who promised to maintain the independence of the papal states. When his first choice, Otto, once crowned, broke his promise and invaded the papal state, Innocent retaliated with excommunication and deposition. His support swung to Frederick II, ruler of Sicily, who promised both to keep Sicily from being joined with Germany and to acknowledge the Pope's authority over the German Church. Frederick's victory against Otto in the Battle of the Bouvines in 1214 thus represented a victory for papal power, for a time.

Innocent had similar success in asserting his power throughout Europe. In England, when King John refused to recognize the archbishop of Canterbury elected by the clergy and tried to impose his own candidate instead, the Pope placed all England under interdict. For six years no religious services except baptisms and funerals were permitted. Finally, in 1213, under threat of invasion by the Pope, now allied with Philip Augustus of France, John gave up his crown, receiving his kingdom back as a vassal of the Pope.

Philip Augustus of France was forced to submit to papal power as well. When that king refused to acknowledge his bride, Ingeborg of Denmark, as wife and queen, Innocent not only refused to grant a divorce but laid an interdict on France. The struggle went on for twenty years, until the king gave in and restored Ingeborg's rights as wife and queen.

The supremacy of papal over secular power that Innocent achieved meant that the Church was in fact a comprehensive supranational society, similar to a state. To administer this society, Innocent reorganized the papal Curia, establishing three separate divisions: the Chancery, dealing with official documents; the Camera, with finances; and the Judiciary, with the law. As one of the greatest legal geniuses to occupy the papal throne, Innocent issued many valuable papal decrees. These decisions ultimately had the force of universal law when they were incorporated into Gregory IX's first collection of Decretals in 1234.

Unfortunately, Pope Innocent's sense of the law did not always find him on the side of justice. In 1215 the Pope's own archbishop sided with the English barons who forced the tyrannical King John to sign the Magna Carta, establishing their right to government by law. But the Pope, looking only at the letter of the law, granted the king's appeal, excommunicated the barons, suspended the archbishop, and declared the Charter invalid.

The desire for civil order that lent Pope Innocent's support to squashing the barons' secular rights reveals the frame of mind that led the same Pope to initiate the infamous Inquisition. Freed from struggles with secular rulers, Innocent turned to impose order within the Church. There the disruptive factor to a unified faith were the Cathari, or heretics, also known as the Albigenses, from the city where many were concentrated. Especially popular in southwest France, the Cathari, like the earlier Manichees, were an ascetic dualistic religious sect who believed in the inherent evil of the material world. When ten years of persuasion failed to eradicate them, their suspected involvement in the murder of a papal agent led Innocent to wage a military crusade. Inhabitants of several Cathar cities were massacred, and at the Battle of Muret the heretics were decisively crushed. To root and stamp out heresy completely, however, Innocent also set up an informal committee with special powers independent of the local church authorities. Gregory IX made the committee a permanent Inquisition in 1233. Although some inquisitors did undoubtedly operate with integrity, the system itself involved anonymous accusations without any advocate for the accused's defense. And in 1251 the papacy endorsed confession by torture.

At the time of the Magna Carta, however, the Pope was undoubtedly absorbed with his great council. This fourth Lateran Council was a call to spiritual reform which brought over twelve hundred clergy to Rome in 1215 for one of the largest and most impressive assemblies of the middle ages. The inquisition was one of several measures to guarantee a unified Christian community. Similar legislation made non-Christians, and especially Jews, wear distinctive dress and forbade their appearance in public during the Holy Week of Easter. The rest of the legislation represents the culmination of Pope Innocent's constant concern to upgrade the standards of all aspects of Christian clerical and lay life. Instructions to the faithful were to be given in the mother tongue rather than Latin. Christians were to make an annual confession and receive the Eucharist each Easter. And the first official declaration of the doctrine of transubstantiation asserted that during the Eucharist the substance of the bread became the body of Christ and the wine his blood.

The picture of the Church that emerges from these decrees reveals some of the changes that took place in the development of the medieval Church. The growth of Christianity to over seventy million followers by the time of Innocent III involved a similar expansion of the clergy. Consequently, the earlier system of bishops and deacons developed into two different ranks of clergy. The bishops in charge of approximately four hundred districts, or dioceses, who came from powerful land-holding families, were subject to the Pope, and sometimes were also civil servants of the king. In addition to the enlarged spiritual, administrative, and judicial duties whose emergence we have seen, these bishops now also supervised a lower rank of clergy. The dioceses were divided into parishes run by secular priests who came from the lower classes. Through a system of councils and visitations the bishops made both the clergy and laity account for their adherence to the discipline and faith of the Church. The priests, on the other hand, much like the earlier deacons, administered such sacraments as baptism, confession, and the Eucharist, and attended to the sick, the poor, and the burial of the dead.

Along with the increased hierarchy within the clergy came an increased separation between clergy and laity. The priest was separated from his parishoners by his rule of celibacy, by his distinctive dress (based on remnants of the imperial toga), and by his use of Latin, a language only the educated could understand, in Church rituals. The effect of this separation on actual worship is most dramatically seen in the difference between the medieval celebration of the Eucharist and earlier practice. What was once a communal meal became a ceremony that the priest performed and the parishioners witnessed, physically separated from the priest by a heavy railing. Since the language was no longer immediately intelligible to the faithful, the Mass, as it was called after the fifth century (probably from the words of dismissal at the ritual's end), came to be a dramatic performance. The emphasis was no longer on the miracle of the resurrection, but on Christ the man, whose suffering and death the priest symbolically acted out. The focus was no longer on the act of blessing the bread and wine. Instead, the high point became seeing the unleavened bread and cup of wine when the priest held them up after consecration. In fact, a warning bell announced this elevation of the host to the parishioners, many of whom went from church to church simply to witness the event. The community's participation in the Mass was restricted to Easter. Then, no longer able to bring their own bread to be blessed, nor to hold the consecrated coin-shaped unleavened bread and cup of wine, the parishioners knelt and received the wafer which the priest placed on their tongue.

Religious Orders and the Spread of Learning

By the twelfth century, in addition to the secular
clergy, roughly two thousand monasteries and convents
housed the "regular clergy," from the Latin term *regula*
for the rule of poverty, chastity, and obedience for
which these clergy withdrew from ordinary life. After
the Cluny reform, these religious houses were grouped
into "orders" under the centralized authority of the
abbot, to whom they owed their absolute obedience,
independent of the local bishop. As a retreat and outlet
for widows and unmarried daughters of the great, sev-
enth- and eighth-century English and Frankish convents were especially notable for the remarkable leadership and religious and literary accomplishments of
such abbesses as Hilda of Whitby and Radegunde of
Poitiers.

By the ninth century, monasticism, incorporated into
the feudal system and drawn from the nobility, became
one of the most important medieval institutions. Monastic schools provided the only effective successors to
the municipal schools of the late Roman Empire. Only
these institutions had the staff and libraries to preserve
Latin and Christian classics. Monks and abbots were
valued educators, friends, and advisors of important
rules. As time passed, however, the monasteries declined. Despite vows of poverty, the monasteries acquired extensive land holdings which they ornamented
with magnificent abbeys and cloisters.

The worldliness and materiality of the predominantly Benedictine monastic orders inspired a move-

ment to return to a more simple piety, and especially to embrace poverty. The Cistercian monastic order, dedicated to these goals, was founded at Citeaux in 1098. In the twelfth century, its most famous adherent, Bernard of Clairveaux, not only inspired his order by his own example, but became the moral consciousness of Western Christendom, rebuking popes and emperors alike. Bernard's dedication of the abbey at Clairveaux to the Virgin Mary, and his mystical approach to spirituality is representative of a new intensely personal piety which was gaining strength within the Church. Undoubtedly inspired by monastic practice, its impact on Church worship can be seen in the increasing emphasis on private prayer and meditation, and on the decreasing emphasis on public penance in favor of private penance and confession.

The twelfth-century spiritual revival took place in a period of uncommon expansion and growth in Western Europe. Relative peace fostered the revival of commerce and shifted the growing population from the country to the towns and cities. In the thirteenth century, partly as a response to these changing conditions, a new kind of religious order emerged. Rather than withdrawing from ordinary life, the friars, from the Latin *fratres*, for "brothers," were dedicated to pursuing monastic ideals while going out into the world, and to converting by preaching and moral example.

Two great mendicant orders, as they were called from their practice of begging alms to support themselves, arose. In Italy, a nobleman, Francis of Assisi (1182– 1226), inspired disciples when he decided to imitate Christ's life, giving up all possessions to travel from town to town, preaching moral repentance, trust, and joy in God's world. Although originally against formal organization, St Francis sought and received papal support when his followers grew. The new order of Friars Minor soon spread throughout Europe, preaching and actively promoting social welfare. In time it became clear that the Franciscans could not support themselves and their projects by begging, and the Pope sanctioned a system that gave mythical ownership of lands and goods to the Pope. This legal fiction divided the Franciscans. The Conventuals believed it necessary, while the Spiritualists demanded a return to the ideals of St. Francis.

In Spain a second great order, the Dominicans, was founded in 1216 by a Castilian nobleman, Dominic de Guzman (1170–1221), to combat the Albigensian heresy. This Order of Preachers, as they were called, differed from the Franciscans in their emphasis on educating the friars. To ensure the success of their preaching, the Dominicans insisted that each house set up its own school with its own master in theology. The Dominicans also radically changed the notion of monastic authority, replacing the abbot's total, lifetime authority by a constitution which provided for democratic election of superiors for short periods of time.

The mendicant orders, which included the less numerous Carmelites and Augustinians, became extremely influential agents of the Pope, to whom they were directly responsible. Immensely popular as preachers and confessors, the friars also established many foreign missions. Most crucial of all, however, was the friars' intimate involvement with the development of learning in Western Europe.

The concentration of population in the urban centers

over the eleventh and twelfth centuries lessened the influence of the monastic schools in favor of the urban schools in Italy and the cathedral schools in northern Europe. A new institution of learning, the university, arose as scholars and students living in the urban areas near these schools formed unions to protect their rights against the local authorities. Since some of these rights involved clerical privilege, the scholars sought and received protection from the Pope. Papal guarantee of the rights of the universities, where the higher studies of medicine (especially at Salerno), law (at Bologna), and theology (at Paris) were pursued, in effect gave the papacy control of the dominant intellectual force of the thirteenth century.

This control became extremely important during the intellectual activity and furor caused by the rediscovery of the works of Aristotle due to increased contact with Spain and the East. Between 1150 and 1250 nearly all of Aristotle's works were translated into Latin, together with Jewish and Arabic commentaries, making Aristotelian thought available to the Western Church for the first time. At first, Aristotle's completely rational interpretation of human experience was perceived as a threat to Christian revelation, and the Church prohibited its teaching in 1210 and 1215. Within a short time, however, it was clear that Aristotle's encyclopedic presentation of Greek knowledge was too crucial to be ignored. The confrontation of the teachings of the Church with Aristotelian thought was worked out in the universities, especially of Paris and Oxford, with the friars of the nearby schools playing a leading role.

Ultimately the Dominicans tended to endorse the scholastic position that reason and faith could be joined. Albertus Magnus (1206–1280) acknowledged the importance of rational knowledge, defending its autonomy within its own sphere. He also helped make Aristotelian thought understood, commenting on it and updating it with his own vast scientific learning, based on observation and experiment.

But it was Albertus's favorite student, Thomas Aquinas (1225–74), who integrated Aristotelian learning with Christian faith. Not by accepting all of Aristotle, but by an ingenious synthesis of Aristotelian, Platonic, and Christian thought, Aquinas developed the first original philosophy since Aristotle. This philosophy, called Thomism, emphasized the senses as a source of human knowledge that could only strengthen Christian faith. It presented a rational understanding of God as the creator and source of all being, goodness, and truth, the uncaused cause in whom alone essence and existence are united. By bringing all aspects of human knowledge to bear on theological issues, Aquinas's great intellectual achievements not only helped change the concept of theology, but also profoundly altered the nature of Western thought.

Aquinas's views did not win immediate acceptance in the medieval Catholic Church, however. Seen as dangerous to a more Augustinian spirituality, his controversial views were often bitterly opposed by such Franciscans as John Peckam (1225–92) and the great leader Bonaventure (1221–74) as well. In 1227 the archbishop of Paris and subsequently the Dominican archbishop of Canterbury as well condemned such Thomist views as the dependence of the soul on the body as heresy, along with the extreme rationalism of such radical Aristotelians as Siger of Brabant (1260–77). Not until the sixteenth century were Aquinas's views accepted as the official Catholic doctrine, which made Thomism synonymous with medieval scholasticism and the Catholic Church.

IV

The Collapse of
Medieval Unity

The Decline of the Papal
Monarchy

THE SUPREMACY OF THE PAPAL MONARCHY AS WORLD
rulers could not be sustained after the death of Innocent III. Ultimately the struggle for power between the
papacy and the very Hohenstaufen emperor Pope Innocent III had endorsed proved the undoing of both papacy and empire. Despite his initial promises, Frederick II (1211–50) became less the Protector than the
oppressor of the Church. In 1227 when Frederick's attacks on the Lombard towns threatened the safety of the

papal states, Pope Gregory IX (1227–41) retaliated with not only excommunication but a declaration of holy war against the emperor. In 1238 European Christendom was torn apart by the brutal fighting between the Guelf party for the Pope and the Ghibelline party for the emperor. Frederick's physical torture of those in the papal party horrified Europe, but the increasing worldliness of papal retaliation through warfare and money undermined papal spiritual prestige as well.

Just as earlier Popes had turned to the Franks, at Frederick's death in 1250 the papacy turned from the Hohenstaufen heirs to Charles of Anjou. This brother of the king of France promised to rule Sicily by keeping it separate from the Empire. The alliance further eroded popular confidence in papal leadership. The papal role in Charles's capture and the elimination of the Hohenstaufen heirs was seen as an unwarranted intrusion of spiritual authority into purely political affairs. In 1281, when a Sicilian popular revolt against French occupation ended Charles's rule, papal support for Charles was interpreted as support for the suppression of freedom.

The election of Pope Boniface VIII (1294–1303) promised to revive the power of Innocent III. His proclamation of the first papal jubilee in 1303 brought more than a million pilgrims to Rome. The clash between Boniface and the rulers of both England and France, however, revealed a new force in European affairs—the rising sense of a national state. Boniface's extreme proclamations of the ultimate supremacy of spiritual over temporal authority in his *Unam Sanctam* of 1302 did not take this new force into account. By the thirteenth century the Church had amassed enormous wealth that the rulers of the emerging national states needed. Disputes over finances in the newly money-centered economy led to expressions of national anti-papal feeling in legislative assemblies of both countries for the first time.

In 1296 Boniface issued *Clericis Laicos*, a bull threatening excommunication for secular rulers levying taxes on the clergy without papal consent. The reactions of Edward I of England (1271–1307) and Philip the Fair of France (1285–1314) were markedly different from the earlier reactions of King John and Philip Augustus to Innocent III. Edward retaliated by declaring the clergy outlaws, outside the protection of secular law, while Philip the Fair prohibited exporting money without royal consent, cutting off French contributions to Rome. The shift in power from Church to king was made graphic in 1303. Threatened with excommunication, Philip did not, like Henry IV at Canossa, stand penitent in the snow. Instead, he sent three hundred horsemen and a thousand foot soldiers to storm the papal palace at Anagni, keeping the eighty-five-year-old Pope captive in his own home.

The papacy proved powerless to condemn Philip's tyranny against the Church. Rather, Boniface's successors were forced to make concessions to Philip to prevent further loss of face. To avoid Philip's threatened posthumous condemnation of Boniface as heretic and anti-pope, among other things Pope Clement V (1305–14) agreed to Philip's brutal destruction of the religious order of the Templars. In 1309 Clement temporarily moved the papal court from Rome to Avignon in southern Provence in order to deal with Philip's machinations. Pressure from conflict in Italy and the papal states, an increased number of French cardinals, intrigues with the French kings, and papal illness prolonged the residency in Avignon until 1378. This Avignon residency, called the Babylonian Captivity by papal opponents, became symbolic of the extent to which the papacy was in effect under the power of the French kings.

During the Avignon residency the papacy consolidated its authority over the Church, reorganizing and centralizing administration by more direct papal control of appointments and benefices. It also tried to combat heresy and reform abuses within the Church. Pope John XXII (1316–34) even expressed disapproval of the papal tendency toward nepotism, or appointing relatives to Church positions. The papacy, however, was attempting to conduct its business in the midst of considerable disorder. The Black Death which began in 1348, the Hundred Years War in France (1337–1453), and civil war in Italy devastated the countryside, depleting and dissipating the ranks of the monasteries as well. In addition, the Popes were without a main source of revenue in the residences and property they left behind in strife-torn Italy. Pressed by their need to finance wars in Italy, to conduct crusades and to build a suitable residence at Avignon, the papacy was forced to expand its already considerably elaborate financial machinery. Consequently it levied a variety of ingenious new taxes and fees.

Much of this money went to worthwhile causes. The Avignon papacy was a staunch patron of the arts, the universities, and the religious orders. But the collection of increased Church taxes enriched the papacy at the expense of the bishops and local churches, causing anti-papal sentiment among both clergy and laity. Politics and national feeling aroused English hostility to paying taxes to a Church strongly influenced by its French opponents in the expensive Hundred Years War. The splendor of the papal court and the sometimes brutal methods of collecting papal taxes, together with increased resistance to financing papal wars felt to be more to retain temporal possessions than spiritual, all contributed to further weakening of papal prestige.

Throughout the Avignon residency such leaders as the dynamic Catherine of Sienna (1347–80) insisted that the papacy belonged in the holy city of Rome. In 1377 Pope Gregory XI (1370–77) finally braved the civil discord in Italy to return to Rome and reestablish residence and authority over the papal states. Unfortunately, however, Gregory died within a year. When his Italian successor, Urban VI (1378–89), turned out to be an irascible tyrant, the cardinals denounced Urban and elected a rival Pope. This Pope, Clement VII (1378–94), immediately returned to Avignon, splitting the Western Church into two camps. The Holy Roman Emperor, England, the Netherlands, Castille, Hungary, and Poland supported Urban, while France and its allies, Scotland, Luxembourg, and Austria rallied to Clement's side. Successors were elected at the death of both Urban and Clement. Thus, the scandal of the Avignon residency was quickly followed by the worse scandal of the Great Schism.

Forty years of that Schism (1378–1417) brought further deterioration to papal prestige. The period was marked by violence. Not only did Pope war against Pope and popes torture cardinals, but increased papal taxes led to increasingly harsher methods of collection.

Negotiations for the joint resignations of both Roman and Avignon popes, Gregory XII (1406–14) and Benedict XIII (1394–23), proved fruitless. Finally, both sides realized the only solution to the crisis lay in the theory of conciliarism, which asserted the supremacy of the council of cardinals over the Pope. Led by Gerson and the University of Paris, the cardinals looked back to the days when such emperors as Constantine had called councils without the consent or expressed will of the Pope. They declared that since the power of the Church lay in the community of the faithful, the decrees of the council that represents that community could be valid, even against the will or without the consent of the Pope.

In 1409 a council representing most of the dignitaries of the Church met at Pisa and declared both Popes schismatic, heretical, and therefore deposed. In their place the Council elected a new Pope, Alexander V (1409–10). When both Roman and Avignon popes refused to step down, however, the situation became worse. Instead of two popes, there were now three. Alexander's subsequent death did not help, for the Council simply elected John XXIII (1410–15) his successor.

The next Council held at Constance in 1414 revealed the strength of the rising forces of nationalism. This Council, summoned by Pope John under pressure from the Holy Roman Emperor Sigismund (1368–1432), included princes as well as representatives of the Church. By extending the vote to laymen and by voting as nations rather than individuals for the first time, this council succeeded in ending the Great Schism. Despite Pope John's attempt to sabotage the Council by leaving

Constance, and the resistance of the Avignon Pope, the Council deposed both. The Roman Pope then resigned, and the Council elected Martin V (1415–49) new Pope of a reunited Church.

After successfully ending the Schism, the Council turned to reform the many abuses created by the Avignon residency and the Great Schism. The financial pressures of this period had brought back some of the worst excesses of the century before Gregorian reform. Simony was prevalent. The nobility again were in control of high Church positions, which they exploited for worldly gain. Increasingly, in order to supplement the income of the clergy, more than one position was given to the same man. These practices created dioceses that never saw their bishops. Pluralism and absenteeism created a loss of morale throughout the Church. Training for the lower clergy was lax, preaching was neglected, and such worldliness as concubinage was again commonplace. The monasteries, ravaged by death and war, were no longer centers of learning. The Benedictine Rule was out of touch with social conditions. Many monks lived outside the cloisters, while those within became increasingly attached to material life.

Reform was hampered by conflicts of interest within the Church hierarchy. The bishops wanted to reform the papacy and the papally controlled regular clergy who were the bishops' rivals. The lower clergy wanted to reform the endowments and privileges of the higher clergy. These divisions, together with conflicting national interests, prevented the Council from instituting any real reform. The Council ended in 1418 with a decree that limited papal powers, condemned simony, and called for regularity in clerical conduct. Actual reform was left to the Pope to enact through negotiation with individual nations and through future councils which he was obligated to call at regular intervals.

Unfortunately, this reform did not come. Pope Martin diverted his own resources into political intrigue as he sought to secure control of the papal states. At his election he had denied the supremacy of council over Pope. The issue came to a head at the Council of Basel in 1431 when the next Pope, Eugenius IV (1431–47), tried to dissolve the council he had called, without accomplishing any reform. At first the Council prevailed. By 1433 its assertion of conciliar supremacy finally forced a reluctant Eugenius to recognize the Council's right to refuse to disband. However, this gain proved short-lived.

The only reform the Council could agree on went too far, stripping the Pope to a figurehead financially dependent on the Council. In retaliation the Pope sought to move the Council to Italy to discuss reunification with the Greek Church. The result was a split in the Council. Although originally a majority voted to stay in Basel, the disorder that ensued swung votes to the Pope's side. Ultimately, only a recalcitrant minority remained at Basel, where they deposed Eugenius and elected the last anti-pope, Felix V (1439–49) in 1439.

Papal support was strengthened when the Greek Church acknowledged the Pope over the Council, and seemed on the verge of reunification with the Church. One by one the key national powers who had remained at Basel swung their support to the Pope. The Concordat of Vienna ended the Basel Council in 1448. The next year Pope Felix resigned. With the help of national political interests, the papacy succeeded in putting down conciliarism, but the idea of enacting reform through a council led by the Pope persisted throughout the fifteenth and sixteenth centuries. The real victory was that of the national states whose increasing authority over the church saw the emergence of national Churches in England, France, and Spain.

The Reformation

The conciliar movement, however, represented an important recognition within the fifteenth-century Church of its need to regain spiritual authority by reforming the abuses that had permeated the Church during the recent period of papal decline. The Council of Basel expressed the view of many that the root of the problem lay in the financial excesses of the papacy, which fostered a climate emphasizing external rather than internal spiritual values. The sale of indulgences became a glaring example of this trend. Beginning around the time of the Crusades, indulgences were granted on the theory that the Church had access to a spiritual treasury of merit upon which its members could draw to lessen the temporal punishment of their sins. These sins were considered already partially repaid by the disproportion between the sins and the actual punishment of Christ and the saints. At first, indulgences were given sparingly, and the need to accompany them with interior repentance and good works, which might include a donation of money, was stressed. During the period of papal decline, however, an increasing number of papal indulgences cheapened their value. By the fifteenth century the emphasis on internal repentance was lost in the association with an exchange of money that seemed to promise nearly automatic salvation in itself. In addition, payments for invocation of the saints, veneration of relics, and elaborate prayers for the dead created a commercialism in the Church that was seen to pander to ignorance and superstition.

The inability of the Church to attain reform because of factions within its hierarchy intensified the feeling that the Church in general was preoccupied with external rights and privileges rather than spiritual and apostolic concerns. The sense that the clergy had over-elaborated devotional practices, together with a breakdown in charity apparent in increasingly open hostility not only between secular and regular clergy but also between such rival religious orders as the Dominicans and Franciscans as well, fueled a growing anticlericalism among the laity.

In fact, the Council of Constance had dealt with several reform movements expressing increasing dissatisfaction with the entire hierarchical structure of the Church. The limits of responsiveness of the fifteenth-century Church to the times can be seen in its reactions to movements led by two scholars who wanted basic spiritual reform. Only the writings of the leader of the Oxford movement, John Wycliffe (1329–84), were burned as heresy in 1382; but the leader of the Wycliffe-inspired Bohemian movement, John Huss (1369–1415), himself was burned at the stake in 1415 for refusing to renounce his views.

Both movements, wanting a return to a simplified biblical Christianity, asserted the ultimate authority of the Bible over the Church. Denouncing canon law, clerical hierarchy, and endowments as unnecessary worldliness, they advocated less emphasis on sacraments and more on preaching to the laity in their own language. Wycliffe's emphasis on the importance of making the Bible available to the laity led to the first English translation of the Vulgate. His works were condemned because of his view that the doctrine of transubstantiation, which asserted that the substance (meaning "essence") of the bread and the wine is miraculously changed into the substance of the body and blood of Christ during the Eucharist, was not only unnecessary because unbiblical, but encouraged popular misunderstanding and superstition.

These concerns for spiritual reform, however, ultimately became connected with assertions of national interest. The English Church did not challenge all papal control, but it did use Wycliffe's arguments to support nonpayment of English tithes to a papacy residing in enemy French territory. Huss's more severe treatment came from the Bohemian movement's development of the truly revolutionary implications in Wycliffite reform. Huss not only stridently denied the authority of an immoral papacy, his advocacy of Czech control of its own Church inextricably fused religious and national freedom. His death, creating a martyrdom which led to a demand for reform by force, posed a threat to the unity of the Church that was answered by military force.

Unfortunately, then, the connection between some national interests and extreme demands for reform allowed even those Church leaders concerned to establish reform to fear that doing so would involve social disorder. Reform was left to the leadership of the Popes. Papal preference for acting alone rather than calling a council was undoubtedly based on fear of further disruption and erosion of papal authority. Conciliarism's serious challenge to that authority continued to be felt. Pope Pius II (1464–71), a former supporter of conciliarism, issued a bull in 1460 condemning appeal of papal action to a council. But Church and secular leaders continued to support the legitimacy of such an appeal up through Luther's time. What was needed to restore papal authority was true resumption of moral and spiritual leadership, but this leadership was not provided by the Renaissance Popes.

Under Popes Sixtus IV (1471–84), Innocent VIII (1484–92), and Alexander VI (1492–1503) some of the worst excesses of the Avignon residency and pre-Gregorian reform returned. Patronage of such artists as Michelangelo, whose works continue to make Rome and the Vatican showplaces of Renaissance achievement, brought external splendor to the papal court, but moral and spiritual leadership were lost to political and worldly ends. The papal states became a leading power in European politics, with the papal court no more spiritual than any other royal court. Church offices were literally bought and sold to further personal and dynastic interests. Under the leadership of Alexander VI and his notorious son Cesare Borgia, the Curia was once again the scandal of Christendom.

Papal authority was also undermined by Renaissance humanism, the intellectual and artistic movement centered on human capabilities, whose rediscovery of Greek language and thought continued the emphasis of Wycliffe and Huss on recovering the historical origins of Christianity. Pope Nicholas V (1447–53), patron of humanist learning who established the Vatican library, and Pope Pius II, a humanist scholar himself, both tried to bring the fruits of humanist learning into the service of the Church. However, the recovery of the Greek New Testament and the writings of the Greek fathers, largely made possible by their translation into Latin by the great Erasmus (1446–1536), pointed to the lack of mention of the papacy in those sources. In addition, the work of humanist scholars such as Lorenzo Valla and Erasmus led to the claim that both the Donation of Constantine and the Isidorian Decretals were forgeries. Discussions of these foundations of papal authority together with humanist criticism of Scholastic philosophy and theology fostered a growing distrust of the Latin tradition of the Church. The invention of the printing press made these criticisms the subject of both learned and popular debate.

The century before the Reformation then saw a growing scrutiny which questioned whether the medieval Church was fulfilling the mission of Christ. The Constantinian concept of the Church as political entity was put into question, and the insertion of Greek and Arabian philosophy into theology was challenged as straying too far from the Christological basis of the earliest Church. There was a growing sense that the medieval Church was no longer fulfilling its role as mediator between Christ and humanity. Renaissance art directed an emotional insistence on the suffering of Christ, the sorrowing of the Virgin Mary, terror of the Day of Judgment, and fear of the Dance of Death. Tired of the struggles of the Avignon residency, the Great Schism, and the quarrels between cardinals and Popes, and vexed by the intricacies of the arguments of the Scholastics, many Catholics simply longed for an intense and personal piety stripped of the excesses of the medieval Church.

Interestingly, an experiment in personal devotional life was approved by the Council of Constantine's endorsement, over the objection of the Dominicans, of the Brethren of the Common Life. This voluntary monastic community was established by the Dutch reformer, Gerard Groote (1340–84), who like Francis of Assisi opposed clerical rule, and any distinction between clergy and laity as well. Like the Franciscans, however, the Brethren undoubtedly owed their survival to their ultimate affiliation with a formal order, in this case the Augustinian monks. The return to inward faith of the Brethren, made famous by Thomas à Kempis's *Imitation of Christ*, proved inspirational to much later reform. Its influence on reform of German monastic life spurred sixteenth-century churchwide reform, just as earlier monastic reform at Cluny spurred later Gregorian reform. Its indirect effect on one German Augustinian monk, Martin Luther (1438–1546), brought the sixteenth-century Church its greatest crisis since the Gospels had been brought to the Gentiles.

Luther entered a very strict monastery in 1505 after having been struck to the ground by lightning. A few years later, obsessed with anxieties about salvation, he suffered an intense spiritual crisis that confession, fasting, and prayer did not ease. Reading Augustine and the Bible, however, led to a mystical revelation, much like those of Augustine and Paul, that brought peace of mind by changing Luther's understanding of what God's justice meant. Luther believed the Augustinean concept of human nature as totally corrupt due to original sin, and that consequently there could be no freedom of will. His fear of an Old Testament God's just punishment of humanity's sinful state was converted to his acceptance of a loving New Testament God whose limitless mercy and generosity justifies, or saves, humanity in spite of its sinful state. Human salvation then is not a matter of human merit, but of the gracious gift of God. For Luther, as for Paul, this salvation comes through faith in God's mercy, rather than good works.

Luther's theology, like that of Wycliffe, reflected the influence of such Nominalist thinkers as William of Ockham (1285–1349), whose revival of the claim that God's omnipotence cannot be known and understood by human reason created an emphasis on personal and emotional faith based on the Bible. Like Paul, Luther did not set out to revolutionize the Church. He spoke initially as a Catholic concerned for spiritual reform. The crisis began with his attack on a flagrant abuse: the sale of an indulgence to the Archbishop of Mainz for blatant commercial rather than spiritual gain. Ostensibly to rebuild St. Peter's Church, the indulgence was actually a means of financial profit for the Archbishop, a banking firm, and the Curia. To make matters worse, when the indulgence was presented to the laity, they were also urged to give money to buy salvation. The Church, however, failed to acknowledge the seriousness of the situation. Luther's famous call to debate the system of indulgences by posting ninety-five theses on the door of the Wittenberg church in 1517 was ignored by his fellow Church leaders. In 1518 Pope Leo X (1513–21), too absorbed in Italian politics to take time out for a "monks' quarrel," charged Luther with heresy, without acknowledging any abuse of indulgences.

Only when Luther's call for a general council was also ignored, did he promote a reformation of the Church that ultimately proved revolutionary. Calling, like the humanists, for a return to the simplified Christianity of the Gospels, he sought to eliminate much that had come to present an obstacle rather than an aid to personal devotion in the German Church. Substituting the authority of the Bible, which he eventually translated into German, for that of the popes, Luther continued the conciliar debate about papal primacy. Ultimately he rejected apostolic succession and emphasized the historical Church as a community of the faithful whose origin was human. Denying the need for separation between clergy and laity, Luther also called for an end to celibacy of priests.

Luther's reform of the Church service emphasized the participation of the congregation. He reemphasized the art of preaching, focusing the service on a sermon addressed to the laity. Luther also composed rousing hymns, which the congregation would sing together. He reduced the sacraments to baptism and the Eucharist, and stripped the Mass to essentials, rejecting the doctrine of transubstantiation. He also made the Mass understandable by translating it into the language of the congregation. Finally, the participants would receive the wine as well as the bread of the Eucharist in their own hands.

Through a series of vigorous public debates and the recently invented printing press, Luther's ideas spread rapidly. Striking a responsive chord for Catholics dissatisfied with the structure and hierarchy of the

Church, his ideas soon won widespread support. Many priests became ex-priests, married, and formed new Protestant congregations which put Luther's reforms into practice. In addition, Luther appealed to German nationalism. He gained the support of the German princes through his encouragement to increase their authority over the German Catholic Church by helping enact reform. Thus, political intervention and the threat of popular revolt kept Luther from the earlier fate of John Huss when, called before the German Diet of Worms in 1521, Luther refused to recant his views.

Ultimately, the political situation fostered the spread of Protestantism. The Emperor Charles V (1519–58), a staunch Catholic committed to stamping out heresy, declared Luther an outlaw. But the German princes, identifying with Luther's cause, refused to act against him. Meanwhile, the increase of new Protestant congregations made it necessary to define their relationship with the existing Church. Fear of revival of conciliarism, of increased imperial strength, and of the hostility of the German princes undoubtedly led the papacy to avoid calling a council. Finally, both imperial and national forces organized militarily. The Protestant princes formed the the Schmalkald League, which Charles recognized in 1532. The failure of his attempts to heal the schism between Catholicism and Protestantism was sealed by the Peace of Augsburg in 1555, when Charles officially recognized both the Catholic and Lutheran faiths in Germany.

Politics also played a part in the rapid spread of Protestantism beyond Germany. By the middle of the sixteenth century European Catholicism embraced less territory than that ruled by Gregory the Great almost a thousand years earlier. Much of Germany, Austria, France, most of the British Isles, and all of Scandinavia had separated from the Church of Rome. Nowhere in Europe was Protestantism accepted against a monarch's wish. The decision ultimately involved greater or lesser authority of the state over the Church and its wealth.

Even before Luther's death, a split emerged in the Protestant movement. Luther's reforms were followed only in the German and Scandinavian Evangelical Church. The Reformed Church in other countries went beyond Luther's conservative reforms. Ulrich Zwingli (1484–1531) established a more democratic, anti-clerical and anti-institutional Lutheranism in Switzerland. His reform Mass celebrated only the memorial presence of Jesus, and he abolished both images and music. John Calvin's (1509–64) adaptation of Zwingli's reforms to every facet of the new industrial and commercial society made Calvinism the most prevalent form of Protestantism. Calvin provided Protestants with a systematic theological exposition of their faith, in which a church-dominated society reversed Luther's subordination of church to state. His famous theory of predestination also reversed Luther's concept of salvation by asserting that God's divine justice allows most to be damned, and His divine mercy allows only a chosen few to be saved. The Anabaptists, meaning "rebaptized," for their assertion that baptism was to be conferred only on believers rather than infants, promoted the most radical religious, economic, and social reforms. They were often persecuted for their strong belief in individual conscience, private inspiration, and separation of church and state. Their modern descendants include Quakers and Baptists.

The most blatantly political acceptance of Protestantism occurred in England. When Pope Clement VII (1523–34) refused to declare his marriage invalid, Henry VIII (1509–47) repudiated papal primacy and was declared head of the Church of England. Henry, a staunch Catholic who had won the title Defender of the Faith for his writing against Luther, wanted the Anglican Church to remain Catholic. Under his son Edward VI (1547–53), however, Parliament adopted a form of Protestantism that retained the episcopal organization and much of the ritual of the Catholic Church.

The Counter-Reformation

The breakup of the unity of western Christendom ultimately spurred the interior spiritual renewal of Catholicism that had been brewing since the fifteenth century. The creation of such groups as the Oratory of Divine Love in Genoa in 1497 continued the persistent quest throughout the development of the Church for spiritual renewal through regular devotion manifested in good works for others. Continuing the experiment of such groups as the Brethren of the Common Life, its membership combined both clergy and laity. The Oratory provided many of the cardinals chosen by Pope Paul III (1534–49) who restored spirituality to the Curia. Their plan for reform of the Church, presented in 1537, began with the reform of the Curia itself, advocating a revolutionary correction of both its financial abuses and the morality of the men chosen to work within it. Later, some of these men extended the reform within the Curia to the bishopric system. Members of the Roman Oratory established an offshoot called the Theatines in 1524, which set the example of bishops dedicated to the pastoral tasks of preaching, visiting the sick, and administering sacraments to the poor of the urban slums. The spirit of renewal in the religious orders is expressed by the organization of the Capuchins in 1525 to return the Franciscans to their original ideals.

Seventeen years after Luther's call, Pope Paul III, persevering in his dedication to reform, was finally able to assemble the much-needed Council of Trent. Over a period of eighteen years (1545–63), under the leadership of a revitalized Curia, this Council established the shape of Catholicism that was to last four-hundred years. The decrees of faith that were the authoritative and definitive answers of the Catholic Church to Luther, Zwingli, and Calvin, remained virtually unchanged until Vatican II.

The Council of Trent drew a sharp line between Protestant and Catholic teaching by its clear reaffirmation of the traditions that Protestantism was rejecting. Denying Luther's concept of the total corruption of human nature by original sin, the Council declared that for Catholics, justification for salvation required not just faith, but hope and charity expressed through good works as well. Against the Protestant assertion of the authority of the Bible alone, the Council asserted that the Bible must be interpreted according to the tradition of the Church Fathers. It also affirmed the validity of its accounts of the beliefs and practices of the apostolic Church.

Emphasizing the necessity of the Church as mediator between Christ and humanity, the Council reasserted the divine authorization of the rituals, or sacraments, through which the Church acts. Confirming a tradition that emerged around 1150 and was expressed at the Council of Florence in 1439, the Council of Trent explained the nature of the sacraments and set their number. These seven sacraments remain the basis of Catholic practice today: baptism (initiation into Christian life), confirmation (entrance into adulthood), the Eucharist (growth, renewal, and strength in Christian life), penance (forgiveness of sins), final unction (preparation for death), orders (empowering ministering to others as priest), marriage (empowering a joint Christian life). A decree that the marriage ceremony was to take place before a priest and two witnesses also declared marriage between a Catholic and a Protestant invalid.

The Catholic reformation also reaffirmed the traditional teaching on transubstantiation and the sacrificial, rather than merely memorial, character of the Mass. To create order out of the many local variations, however, a decree of 1570 imposed a universal format, the *Missale Romanum*, which remained unchanged until the 1960s. This Tridentine (from *Tridentum*, an old word for the city of Trent) Mass instilled a sense of tradition that emphasized the universality of Catholic doctrine. However, together with the lack of the use of the vernacular, or other changes that would incorporate the laity more, the new rubrical Mass also created the danger of rigidity.

Similarly, in addition to its doctrinal decrees, the Council of Trent led to regulations to protect the faithful from the erroneous doctrines of Protestantism. To insure a better-educated clergy, seminaries were erected to train future priests. To prevent the spread of heresy, the "Index of Forbidden Books" was instituted. Both measures were intended to be temporary, but the Index was not lifted until 1978. Unfortunately, by encouraging academic and spiritual development of the clergy in isolation from the everyday world of the laity, the seminaries sharpened the separation between the two. Both measures also cut off Catholic clergy and laity from mainstream intellectual life.

Thus, the Council of Trent bequeathed a highly centralized and authoritarian Church to modern Catholics. Fears of conciliarism were laid to rest with the acknowledgment of the divine institution of its priestly hierarchy. Papal supremacy was restored. The absolute control of the bishops over their dioceses was strengthened to promote reform. Under the vigorous leadership of such men as Charles Borromeo (1538–84) bishops were ordered to set a good moral example, to reside in their dioceses, to preach regularly, to hold synods and visitations, and to root out concubinage.

The Council of Trent was a pivotal event in the Catholic Reformation whose affirmation of tradition emphasized the stability and universality of the Catholic Church. The papacy emerged from the Council with a restored strength. Much of the Council's success was due to the renewed leadership of Popes Paul III, Julius III (1550–55), and Pius IV (1559–65), who presided over its successive sessions. The restored papacy proved worthy of its regained trust by continuing the work of reform that the Council had only begun.

Pope Paul IV (1555–59) had preferred direct papal action to reassembling the Council. His enforced observance of old and disregarded laws purged the papacy of its worldly bent with lasting effects. Under his rigorous rule many papal fees, multiple benefices, and widespread nepotism were abolished. After Trent, the high standard of papal morality set by Pope Pius V (1566–72) transformed the Vatican into a kind of monastery, from which it never suffered serious relapse. His successors, Popes Gregory XIII (1557–85) and Sixtus V (1585–90) continued to guarantee the enforcement of Trent's decrees. They reorganized the Curical administration, uprooted simony, and supervised the reform of the religious orders. They also cooperated with the Catholic monarchs in wars such as the Spanish Armada in an attempt to replace such newly established Protestant regimes as that of Elizabeth I of England (1558–1603).

The Catholic Reformation also owed its success to the extraordinary vitality of the newly established Society of Jesus, organized in 1534 by the Spanish mystic and former soldier, Ignatius Loyola (1491–1556), and recognized by the Pope in 1540. Their dedication to serving God under the specific authority of the Pope made the Jesuits extremely effective agents of the Church. Jesuit insistence on a life of activity based on a profound interior spiritual life greatly influenced the shape of modern Catholicism. While their long and rigorous training period emphasized self-discipline and military obedience, Jesuits exhibited an unusual flexibility. Reexamining religious traditions, they dispensed with the practice of common prayers in favor of a broad range of activities that enabled them to reach people at all levels. The Jesuits' success in preaching, teaching, providing retreats, and in establishing colleges and missions undoubtedly accounts for their rapid expansion. By the end of the sixteenth century they had thirteen thousand members. They remain the largest and most influential religious order in the Catholic Church today.

The Jesuits became especially influential as educators and missionaries. Establishing colleges whose principal function was to carry on teaching as a form of charity became an extremely effective means of bringing people back to the Catholic Church. Peter Canisius (1521–97) is often called the second Boniface, for his restoration of Catholicism to much of German-speaking Europe in this way. Others had similar success in recovering the Netherlands, Poland, and central Europe. The Jesuits also played a prominent role in the intellectual revival in the Catholic universities. Their defense of traditional faith against the Protestants led to the official endorsement of the great Scholastic Thomas Aquinas as Doctor of the Church in 1567.

The Jesuit emphasis on actively striving for virtue and self-control through an energetic pursuit of good works and an intense meditative form of prayer represents the essence of the revitalized spirituality of the Tridentine Church. The Tridentine emphasis on the sacraments as instruments of God's grace, which balanced this emphasis on individual activity, resulted in a more active participation of the congregation. Devout Catholics now began to confess their sins frequently, rather than once a year as in the medieval Church, and to receive Communion once a week.

The new spirituality was also expressed through other new orders that were extremely influential in establishing reform. In 1575 Philip of Neri (1515–95) established the Oratorians, a community of secular priests who helped create a new spirituality in the officials of the Curia. Neri is sometimes called the Apostle of Rome because of the religious awakening he inspired among all classes in Rome by frequenting crowds, holding informal meetings for the young, giving concerts of religious music, visiting the ill, and establishing vernacular prayers. In Spain the amazing energy and good nature of Theresa of Avila (1515–82) not only brought reform to her Carmelite order but also brought an astonishing revival of religious fervor to all classes. Her writings, considered literary masterpieces, brough mysticism to the masses and made her the first woman to be honored as Doctor of the Church in 1970. The preaching of Francis of Sales (1567–1622), a key figure in the reformation in France, is credited with bringing many Protestants back to the Church. He was instrumental in the reform of the Cistercian abbey Port-Royal, which became famous for its pious and disciplined nuns; with his disciple Jan de Chantal, he founded the less austere Order of Visitation for women. Vincent de Paul (1580–1660) brought about renewed spirituality in the French court. Directing attention to the poor of Paris, he became the founder of organized charity in France.

In addition to the recovery of Catholicism in Europe, the revival of Catholic spiritualism saw an expansion of overseas missions that made up in numbers for the losses to the Protestants. Catholic priests accompanied the explorers who opened up the New World to Europe. New missions were established on the African coast. Missions established in America in 1511 became the center for the conversion of Central and South America. Although there had been earlier attempts to establish missions in the Far East, the modern Catholic missionary movement really took root in 1542 with the mass conversions of the Jesuit Francis Xavier (1506–52) in India, Indonesia, and Japan. Toward the end of his life Xavier realized that the future success of missions depended on a more adaptive attitude toward the anciently established native cultures and traditions. The Jesuit Matteo Ricci (1552–1610) established a Chinese mission in 1581 which was later controversial because of his toleration of the continuation of semireligious rites by Chinese converts. In India, work similar to Ricci's was begun by the Jesuit Robert de Nobili (1577–1656), who adopted the lifestyle of the Brahmins. The missions in Japan and China ran into difficulties, however, and were not resumed until the nineteenth century. The most successful Catholic missionary effort in Asia took place in the Philippines. From a mission established in 1581, the present population numbers about 80 percent, or twenty million Catholics. In addition to the problems of adaptation, the Catholic missions ran into political problems associated with the colonial ambitions of the Catholic rulers who were their patrons. In 1662 the Pope took an important step to alleviate this situation, establishing the Congregation for the Propagation of the Faith, which centralized all mission activities under his control.

The Council of Trent and the spiritual revival it spurred helped create a strong and self-confident seventeenth-century Catholic Church. The reaffirmation of medieval tradition left an authoritarian and rigorous Church but it was clearly also a dynamic spiritual force. It looked out on a different world, however. The end of the religious wars in France and Germany declared a new era. The Edict of Nantes (1598) declared freedom of conscience for all subjects of France. The Treaty of Westphalia (1648) gave Catholics, Lutherans, and Calvinists equality before the law in Germany. The unity of medieval Christendom was forever gone.

V

The Modern Church

Old Problems in a Changing World

BY THE MIDDLE OF THE SEVENTEENTH CENTURY IT WAS clear that a new way of looking at the world was being forged. Many of the original thinkers who contributed to the movement ultimately known as the Enlightenment began within the Catholic Church. On the verge of death in 1543, Nicholas Copernicus (1473–1543) dedicated to Pope Paul III the publication of his theory that the earth revolved around the sun. Since sixteenth-century Church doctrine was based on Scholastic philosophy, which accepted the Aristotelian concept of an earth-centered universe, Copernican theory threatened to undermine the very foundations of the Church. It presented a crisis to the Church similar to the rediscovery of Aristotelian philosophy, which had been seen as a threat to scriptural revelation in the thirteenth century. Just as the earlier Church had initially reacted by attempting to condemn Aristotelian thought, in 1616 the Church denounced the work of Galileo (1564–1642), another Catholic innovator who confirmed Copernican thought. In 1633 the Inquisition brought Galileo to trial, forcing him to recant his views. Thus, the Tridentine Church assumed a reactionary posture, concerned to condemn and repress, rather than to accommodate itself to the new world view.

Like Galileo, René Descartes (1506–1650) personally combined devotion to Roman Catholicism with commitment to the spirit of critical inquiry, demonstrating how reason and logic could confirm religious faith. Ultimately, however, the critical rationalism which he evolved was used to continue the attack begun by the humanists on Scholastic and Church reliance on authority and tradition. This challenge was opposed by the Jesuits but support by such Oratorians as Richard Simon (1638–1712), who, like some humanists before him, tried to show how the spirit of critical inquiry could be used to support Catholic tradition. His *Critical History of the Old Testament*, written in 1678, raised questions about traditional assumptions of biblical authorship and history. These questions were meant to demonstrate the error of Protestant reliance on the Bible alone, and the need for Catholic tradition as well, but the Church authorities, alarmed at the possibilities of departure from interpretation by the Church Fathers, which his method opened up, quickly condemned Simon's work.

Continuing a critical strain heard during the Reformation, Enlightenment philosophy tended to see the Church emphasis on the external authorities of tradition and the Bible as a detraction from the more proper emphasis on personal choice which must be the basis of religious commitment. Feeling that this commitment should be based on a combination of reason and faith—the result of teaching, persuasion, and prayer—rather than coercion, Enlightenment philosophy also stressed tolerance of different religious beliefs. The Catholic Church, on the other hand, continued to uphold the belief that social order depended on religious unity. Its success in detecting and suppressing heresy led it to be seen as an archaic institution that supported bigotry and intolerance. The fact that the post-Reformation Church tended to emphasize the "mystery" of religion in its sacramentalism, veneration of saints, especially Mary, and its refusal to translate the Mass into the vernacular increased the gulf between the Church and Enlightenment thinking.

The increasing confidence in the powers of human reason, which the Enlightenment came to represent, ultimately challenged many of the basic assumptions of the Church. Tracing moral evil back to original sin seemed to contradict common sense and reason. Looking at the material progress evident in the growth of the seventeenth and eighteenth centuries led to the replacement of the idea of a lost golden age with the optimistic notion of progress. Human beings were born naturally good, and with powers of reason that could ensure an increasingly better life with each passing age. Such evils as war, crime, and superstition were all the result of ignorance. The combination of education along rational principles and improved scientific methods would undo these ills and create the best of all possible worlds here on earth.

In England the Deists finally advocated a "natural" religion based on reason. Claiming that the existence of an orderly universe was enough to denote the existence of God, they radically attacked the need for biblical revelation, prophecies, and miracles. The most famous Deist attacks came from France, where such writers as Voltaire (1694–1778) and Diderot (1713–84) continued the humanist tradition of employing rapier wit to attack virtually every institution of the Church. The Jesuits, whose education both Voltaire and Diderot had received, often led the defense of Church tradition.

In fact, during the seventeenth and eighteenth centuries, France became the center of disputes within the Church as well as of debates between the Church and its opponents. The Jansenist controversy, which became centered in France, continued the debate about the nature of original sin, and its relationship to free will and grace, which had been an important part of the Reformation. In 1653 the Pope condemned Jansen's revival of the Augustinean concept of the radical corruption of human nature by original sin as too close to Calvinism. The Jansenists maintained that everything purely natural is evil and that grace is given only to a chosen few. These positions were in part an attack on the Thomistic theology of the Jesuits. The Jansenists endorsed an austere moral life in opposition to the lax morality which they felt the more optimistic Jesuit view of human nature involved. In contrast to Jesuit practice of frequent reception of Communion and confession, the Jansenists felt that reception of Communion should be limited to a rare reward for extreme virtue.

An intellectual and social elite associated with the rigorous convent of Port-Royal provided strong and influential support for Jansenism. Such Jansenist defenders as Blaise Pascal (1623–62), who argued that the Jesuits preached an easy morality in order to gain power over the masses, managed to damage severely the reputation of the Jesuits for a time. In 1693 the publication of a new Jansenist manifesto and vernacular New Testament, however, saw a successful counter-attack by the Jesuits. In 1705 a papal bull condemned the new Jansenist tenets and the king of France levelled Port-Royal to the ground. The Jansenists disintegrated to a small sect within Catholicism. The influence of the Jansenist strain in the Irish Church, however, can be seen in the attitude toward sex and morality that the Irish Catholics brought over to the American Catholic Church.

Jansenism ultimately shaded into Gallicanism, a French movement to restrict papal authority that revived many of the conciliarist theories of the Council of Constance. Gallicans insisted on the independent authority of the bishops as representatives of the Church. They denied separate and personal papal infallibility. They felt that infallibility belonged to the whole Church, and could be expressed either through a general council or through papal decisions that received the consent of the Church.

Gallicanism was part of a European trend toward an

alliance between the state and the national churches. Together with greater autonomy for national churches, Gallicanism sought more limited papal authority over temporal rulers. The French movement reached its peak in the attempt of King Louis XIV (1643–1715) to extend his powers to appropriate Church revenues and appoint bishops. The clash that resulted between the king and Pope Innocent XI (1676–89) led to the declaration of Four Articles in 1682 which became the byword of Gallicanism. In these Articles the French clergy declared that the Pope had only spiritual authority, that his decrees would need the consent of a council of the entire Church, and that he had no separate papal infallibility. Despite a compromise reached after Pope Innocent's death, in which Louis agreed not to require the Four Articles to be taught, Gallican thinking continued to be prominent in the universities and seminaries. The question of papal infallibility was not directly addressed and became an important issue in the First Vatican Council of 1869–70.

Gallicanism dominated Church-state relationships throughout the eighteenth century. Its German counterpart, called Febronianism after the pen-name of Nicholas von Hontheim (1701–90), went beyond the Four Articles to attack papal primacy as well. Febronius declared that papal primacy is in fact an administrative rather than jurisdictional office, that jurisdiction belonged to the Church as a whole, and that primacy was not necessarily attached to the see of Rome. Moreover, declaring that the Popes had gradually usurped powers from the bishops, Febronius invited Catholic rulers to resist papal decrees, and bishops to seek protection from civil rulers against the Pope. Despite papal condemnation of Febronianism, and Febronius's ultimate, if weak, disavowal, his ideas were highly influential. In 1796 the electors of Cologne, Mainz, and Treves made a public proclamation of their grievances against the Roman Curia for its usurpations of their jurisdiction.

The Austrian version of Febronianism was Josephism, which became synonymous with state interference with the Church. Emperor Joseph II of Austria (1765–90) forbade bishops to receive papal decrees, communicate with Rome, or issue pastoral letters without his consent; closed religious orders and monasteries, rearranged parishes; and interfered with every aspect of the service in order to institute his reforms.

The spirit of Gallicanism then was symptomatic of the recurrent struggle between Church and state. Political factors added to the decline in papal prestige, which the Jansenist and Gallican attacks on papal spiritual authority emphasized. Rival secular interests of the Catholic Bourbon and Hapsburg rulers of France, Spain, and Austria contributed to the election of a succession of weak eighteenth-century popes. Temporal rulership of the Papal States continued to involve those popes in political alliances that detracted from their spiritual mission. The disparity between the pomp and ceremony of the Curia and the actual poverty and weak administration of those Papal States combined to make European intellectuals see the Roman Catholic Church as out of touch with changing political and social structures.

As spokesmen for the papacy, the Jesuits defended philosophy and theology that also did not keep up with changing times. Although they had been the most respected educators in the seventeenth century, they failed to keep up with new insights in the sciences. In addition to theological differences with the Jansenists, Jesuit loyalty to the Pope together with their influence as confessors to temporal rulers created many political enemies. The weakness of the eighteenth-century papacy can be seen in the intrigues which ultimately led to the suppression of the Jesuit order.

Ironically, Jesuit missionary work ran into trouble because of what could be called radical politics. In addition to the condemnation of their adaptation of earlier practices into Chinese Christianity, the Jesuits were chased out of their mission in Portugese-controlled Paraguay for their attempts to protect the Indians from commercial exploitation. In 1759 all Jesuits in Portugal were arrested and most were expelled to the Papal States. The financial collapse of their Martinique mission gave the excuse for confiscation of all Jesuit property in France in 1764. The suppression of the Order in France was quickly followed by its suppression in Spain. Although Pope Clement XIII (1758–69) defended the Jesuits in 1765, political pressures led Pope Clement XIV (1769–74) to suppress the entire Order in 1773.

Despite internal disputes, however, on the eve of the French Revolution which transformed the Western world by its enactment of many of the values of Enlightenment thought, the Roman Catholic Church held a strong position in European society. The Constantinian alliance of Church and state gave the clerical hierarchy similar status and privileges to the nobility. In France, where Catholicism was the only form of public worship officially allowed, the clergy formed a powerful First Estate. They were freed from much economic and legal control by their great land holdings, their ability to tithe, their exemption from taxation, and their separate legal system. At the same time they were in charge of most education and social services.

Nevertheless, the French clergy helped create the Revolution by voting against the nobility with the Third Estate to hold a National Assembly in 1789. The clergy helped the Revolution by agreeing to give up their privileges of tithing, and by allowing confiscation of Church property and suppression of religious orders. Catholicism remained the official form of worship. The French Church became a department of state; the clergy, paid civil servants. Despite clerical protests, however, Protestants and Jews were given civil rights as well.

The French clergy were also in favor of the state enacting reform of the Church. They were prepared to accept a certain amount of reorganization, especially to eliminate abuses. Reform shaded into revolutionary overthrow of Church hierarchy, however, when proposed revision of the election system would no longer require bishops' approval of parish priests, nor the Pope's prior approval of the election of bishops. The break came when the clergy were required to sign an oath agreeing to this reorganization or give up their offices, without being allowed to consult within the Church through a council, and before they could receive word from the Pope. The result was a schism within the French Church between the constitutional clergy who took the oath, many only as a matter of form, and the majority of nonconstitutional or nonjuring clergy, who refused the oath, maintaining allegiance to Rome. The split divided towns, villages, and families.

Since the reorganization deprived the Pope of control of the internal affairs of the French Church, the spiritual sovereignty of Rome was at stake. Some nonjuring clergy were bishops who allied with the nobility in opposition to the aims of the Revolution. Fear of this alliance made the National Assembly refuse to allow a Church council to be called. Many of the nonjurors, however, were lower clergy strongly committed to the revolutionary goals. They exposed themselves to prison, exile, and possible death because they felt the Constitutional government had exceeded its temporal authority. Refusal to sign the oath was increasingly associated with disloyalty to the Revolution. Since the king had shown sympathy to the nonjurors, his flight from the Revolution, together with foreign invasions on his behalf led to persecution of the nonjurors as traitors. Harmony between the loyal constitutional clergy and the state ended with the overthrow of the monarch as well, since many of the clergy opposed execution of the king.

Loyalty to the Revolution and patriotism increasingly took on the appearance of a religion itself. Patriotic names replaced religious names, and revolutionary heroes, those of saints. Tension increased between revolutionary and Christian values. Marriage became an issue and test of loyalty to the state. Celibacy was denounced as non-egalitarian and procreation was declared necessary for the survival of the state. In 1793 a Republican calendar replaced the Gregorian one. Dating was based on the birth of the Republic in 1792 rather than on the birth of Christ. A ten-day week replaced the seven-day week and Christian Sunday, and all religious holidays were abolished. The de-Christianizing phase of the Revolution sought to replace the "superstition" and "tyranny" of religion by the cults of reason and feeling.

A violent anti-Christian campaign led by the former oratorian Fouché (1759–1820) and the journalist Hébert (1757–94) culminated in the closing of the churches and the installation of an actress on the high altar of Notre Dame as both a masterpiece of nature and the goddess of reason. The persecution of the Church involved desecration of Church vestments, images, and buildings, and the denunciation of priests as power-hungry hypocrites. Marriages became civil contracts and funerals became civil ceremonies. Catholicism, which remained especially strong in the provinces, was forced underground everywhere. Many priests defrocked themselves. Among the four thousand priests who married, however, were many who simply went through an empty ceremony with their housekeepers in order to survive.

Napoleon's Italian campaign in 1796, however, brought the Revolution in conflict with the Pope. Although Napoleon's Treaty of Tolentino recognized the sovereignty of the Pope over the Papal States, ultimately the French occupied Rome and, fearing Austrian aid, removed the eighty-year-old Pope Pius VI (1775–99) to France, where he died. Both the new Pope, Pius VII (1800–23), and Napoleon, recently proclaimed First Consul (1799–1815), however, saw the benefit of mutual support. Napoleon was especially aware of the power of the Church over France. The Church, on the other hand, after suffering the most severe persecution since the Roman Empire, not only in France, but in Belguim, Germany, England, Ireland, and Poland as well, could use protection. Thus, Napoleon became the new Constantine and Protector of Western Christianity through the Concordat of 1801. Signed with great ceremony at the Cathedral of Notre Dame, this agreement became the model for relationships between the Church and state throughout the nineteenth century.

The acknowledgment of Napoleon by the archbishop who welcomed him at the great West door symbolized this new relationship. In return for recognizing the Church as the religion of the majority of the French, the state was to keep all confiscated property and the clergy were to be paid by the state. The schism between the constitutional and nonjuring clergy was ended by having all bishops resign. The First Consul would then name new bishops, whom the Pope would install and also be able to depose. Centralization of the Church hierarchy was increased as control of the lower clergy was returned to the bishops, rather than to private patrons. Napoleon ensured his further control of the Church by requiring the Gallican articles of 1682 to be taught, and by subjecting the Church to whatever police regulations might be necessary to maintain public order.

The policy of mutual support seemed ensured when Pope Pius traveled to Paris to anoint Napoleon Emperor in 1804. But the Concordat was also proof that the Church was not dependent on any particular kind of political regime or alliance. Confrontation between Emperor and Pope arose when the Pope insisted on the political neutrality of the Papal States and refused to enter into a military alliance against England. Napoleon retaliated by invading and seizing the Papal States. The Pope in turn excommunicated Napoleon. But Napoleon met more than one Waterloo. Despite being held captive by an Emperor who was at the height of his powers for almost six years, the Pope stood firm. He turned his deprivations into an embracement of a monk-like existence. He also used the weapon of refusing to install any bishops until the Papal States were restored, and he was freed. In 1814 a triumphant and unbowed Pope returned to Rome.

The Struggle for Political and Intellectual Freedom

Although the Congress of Vienna of 1814–15 disavowed Napoleon and the Revolution, and restored the old order, putting the Bourbons back on the throne of France, Spain, and Naples, the world to which the Pope returned was fundamentally changed. The Pope was restored as absolute monarch of the Papal States, which stretched from the mouth of the Po River to Ancona on the Adriatic coast of Italy and down to just south of Rome on Italy's western shore. But their security was threatened by the Austrian occupation of the northern states and the move toward a united and independent Italy. The reorganization of territories also meant that the Catholics in Germany, Poland, and Belgium became minorities under the rule of Protestant kings. Even within the Catholic nations, the life of the Church was not the same. Europe and its colonies could never return to an alliance of Church and state based on permanent hierarchies.

Although de-Christianization had failed, its legacy

was anticlericalism. In Spain and Latin America, state-appointed bishops and the Church hierarchy would be overthrown together with the secular government. In France there was still bitter schism. Church property was taken over by the state, and monasteries and seminaries were dismantled. Moreover, the secularization of education and marriage, and the institution of civil divorce meant that the Church had a less firm hold over the daily lives of the people.

Nevertheless, papal power was revived. For the Revolution had also freed the Church from Gallican monarchs and enlightened despots who interfered with the papal elections, tried to coopt Catholic missions to colonial aims, and installed puppet bishops. The fact that Napoleon and Pope Pius alone decided the fate of the French Church set a powerful precedent, and the Pope's strong moral stand against the Emperor enhanced papal prestige.

Undoubtedly influenced by a desire to ensure the social order that was necessary to revive and nourish the growth and renewal of the Church, the Pope allied with the restored monarchies. His renewed moral and spiritual prestige allowed his brilliant Secretary of State, Cardinal Consalvi (1757–82), to strike bargains with most of the restored governments. Agreements similar to that of the Concordat of 1801 ensured the rights and liberties of the Church through most of Europe. Bulwarked by these promises of stability, the Church began an astonishing spiritual regeneration. The Jesuit order was reestablished in 1814. It quickly gained thousands of new recruits and extended throughout most of Catholic Europe. Many more sentimentally oriented new religious orders such as the

Marianists and Society of the Sacred Heart formed and
helped repopulate the empty seminaries. The Society
of Foreign Missions was reestablished in 1815, and
soon provided a century richer than any other in the
formation of new Orders and Sisterhoods, such as the
Oblates of the Blessed Virgin Mary Immaculate and the
Salesians, devoted largely to missionary work. At home
and abroad the spiritual renewal brought many Catholics back to lives of prayer, sacrifice, and the practice of
Christian virtue.

Many intellectuals turned to Catholicism in rejection
of the philosophical scepticism and rationalism of the
Enlightenment. They found its faith in the goodness of
human nature and progress to be superficial and sim-
plistic, and sought to incorporate mystery, tradition,
and faith in their lives. This revolt against reason became a bond between Catholicism and the Romantic
movement. Such Romantic works as Chateaubriand's
The Genius of Christianity (1802), showing a new interest in the aesthetic contributions of the Church, were
highly influential in the Catholic revival. On the other
hand, the conversion to Catholicism late in life of the
extremely important Romantic philosopher Friedrich
Schlegel (1772–1829) revealed the relationship between Romanticism, Catholicism, and reactionary politics.

Not surprisingly, the alliance of the Church with the
restored legitimate governments became an alliance
with political repression. Throughout Europe, the
period after the Congress of Vienna became a time for
hunting down and rooting out any vestige of the Enlightenment ideals which the French Revolution
sought to enact. Liberalism, a philosophy of the new

middle-class concerned with representative government with written guarantees of such personal freedoms as that of religion, became a danger to the social
order of the state. The Age of Metternich and the
Hapsburgs from 1815–48 was an age of secret police,
censorship of books, and strict control of the universities, forcing holders of liberal views underground.
Because liberals tended to be rationalists opposed to
Church control over such matters as marriage and education, they were a danger to the Church as well.

Even the Church, however, had to be embarassed by
the extremist reaction in Spain where the Inquisition
was reestablished, arrests were made, and lands confiscated by Napoleon were turned back to the aristo-
crats and the Church. Because of the anticlerical element involved in the Revolution, the French Church
was only too glad to burn such works as Voltaire's or to
require public oaths of loyalty to the new regime. But
much that was good about the Revolution was thrown
out too. After the death of Pope Pius VII in 1823, the
abolition of all innovations introduced into the Papal
States by Napoleon meant the end of vaccinations and
the return of the Jews to ghettos.

Similarly, the support of repression to maintain social order often meant that the Church did not help its
own. In the revolts of the thirties the Church did support the bloodless emancipation of the English and
Irish Catholics from restrictions that had kept them
from holding public office. However, it did not at first
support the revolt of the Catholic Belgians for independence from a Protestant ruler who interfered in their
religion. Nor did it support the revolt of the Polish
Catholics for freedom from the Orthodox Russian Czar.

The incomprehensibility of such complete Church support for the *status quo* became a focal point for a rising move to incorporate some aspects of liberalism into Catholicism. This move to Catholicize rather than ostracize liberalism challenged the newly revived Church with its need to adjust to a changed post-revolutionary world. The impetus for the movement was a French convert and priest, Felicité de Lamennais (1782–1834), whose writings combined the romanticism and revolutionary power of Chateaubriand and Rousseau. Lamennais felt that the problems of the Church were the result of its alliance with the state. Rather than protecting the Church, he felt that the support of the nobility had separated the Church from the people, blinded it to their oppression, and perverted its mission.

With prophetic fervor, he outlined a plan for separation of the Church from the state, and alliance with the Fourth Estate or the people. He felt that revelation of the truth lay with the people, and support for the people should be shown by support for freedom. Since the revolutionary causes of the 1830s were those of truth and justice, the Church should give its full support to democratic movements everywhere. Once basic suffrage was achieved, the Church could only gain from support of further freedoms. Freedom of the press would ensure the power of the truth better than censorship. Freedom of religious education would ensure religious freedom and freedom of thought.

In 1831, with the help of his friends Count Montalembert (1810–70) and Father Lacordaire (1802–61), Lamennais founded a daily newspaper called *L'Avenir* or "*The Future*," to promote these ideas. Not surprisingly, however, while he won the support of intellectuals and revolutionaries, he won only the ire of the French Church hierarchy. Lamennais was accused of trying to subject the Church to poverty and ruin, and *L'Avenir* was banned from the Church, causing its financial ruin.

Lamennais, however, was strongly influenced by Joseph Le Maistre (1754–1821), whose work *Du Pape* (1819) advocated separation of Church and state by reasserting papal supremacy over all temporal rulers. Thus, Lamennais subscribed to the theory called ultramontanism, or "looking beyond the mountains," that is the Alps, to the strong leadership of the Pope in Rome. And so, together with Lacordaire and Montalembert, he decided to appeal to the Pope in Rome. Unfortunately, the timing was not good. In Rome, Pope Gregory XVI (1841–46), who believed very strongly in Catholic hierarchy and obedience, had just put down the Carbonari revolution, involving terrorization and assassination of papal officials. The Pope's response to Lamennais in 1832 was his *Mirari Vos*, a thorough condemnation of *L'Avenir*, together with a denunciation of liberal Catholicism as absurd, injurious, and perverse. Not surprisingly, in time, Lamennais, clearly a man ahead of his time, came to denounce the Church hierarchy and ultimately left the Church.

Lamennais's ideas did not die, however. Liberal Catholicism continued under the moderate leadership of Montalembert and Lacordaire. Both men were famous speakers who gained supporters by working within the system. Lacordaire, whose famous preaching at Notre Dame had spurred the Catholic revival, also revived the Dominican order in France. He was elected to the Assembly of the Second Republic of France as a liberal Catholic representative of the people, rather than a privileged clergyman. Through Montalembert's continued efforts the Church won control of education in France. One of his strongest supporters, Frederic Ozanam (1913–53), founded the Society of St. Vincent de Paul to aid the poor.

In the meantime the liberals had seen success in the Catholic emancipation that resulted from the revolts of the thirties. The increase of secular liberal strength against the repressive restoration governments could be felt in the South American revolution and in the installation of the liberal French monarch, Louis Philippe (1830–45). The Church had ultimately endorsed the emancipated Catholic regimes, and it supported the moderate new regime in France as less dangerous than a more radical revolution. Pope Gregory XVI had taken advantage of the political and economic situation in the thirties and forties to expand Catholic missions. In addition to the renewed missions in the Eastern Mediterranean, India, and China, the American mission flourished. The Irish immigration in the 1840s brought the Catholic population to nearly a million, causing the metropolitans of Oregon City, St. Louis, New York, Cincinnati, and New Orleans to be added to those of Baltimore.

In 1846 the new Pope, Pius IX (1846–78), showed great promise of liberal sympathies. He began by granting amnesty to Italian nationalists who had been imprisoned and exiled by his predecessor. He also threatened Metternich's troops with excommunication for violating Church property, causing their withdrawal from an attempted occupation of northern Italy. Within a short period of time, Pio Nono, as the Pope was affectionately known, won immense personal popularity. He was looked upon as an exemplary ruler who would ally the Church with the cause of democracy everywhere.

In 1848 the world seemed close to democracy. Revolutions in Sicily and France led to new constitutions. Pope Pius granted a constitution to Rome. He also set up a representative lay assembly to help govern the Papal States. Prince Metternich was overthrown. There was great optimism that the Church was in tune with the changing times.

The times were not quite right for Catholic liberalism, however. Although Pope Pius had stood up to Metternich, in 1848 he refused to give the support of the Papal States to an Italian nationalist war against Catholic Austria. As a result, Pope Pius was accused of deserting the Italian movement for liberation and unification. Demonstrations and riots broke out in Rome. The Pope's Prime Minister was stabbed and killed, and the Pope was kept a virtual prisoner in his palace. Disguised as a simple priest, Pio Nono was forced to escape to Gaeta in Naples. The extremists invited the nationalist revolutionaires Garbaldi (1807–82) and Mazzini (1805–72), who were both anticlerical, to Rome. The Revolutionary Roman Republic they set up invoked a new religion of humanity and progress based on a synthesis between God and the people, without the Church. The Pope called from Gaeta for the Catholic powers to aid him. Even revolutionary France was shocked at the way he had been ousted. In 1850, with the help of the French, the Pope was restored to Rome.

Not incomprehensibly, the restoration of the Pope to

Rome marked a change in the Pope's attitude towards liberalism. After his experience with revolution in Rome, he allied with those who associated liberalism with the anticlericalism of the French Revolution. These opponents of liberalism tended to be political conservatives who saw in liberalism a Satanic influence that created a gulf between the Church and the modern world. They were called integralists because they sought a close alliance with any regime that would unite the Church with the state. By the mid-eighteen-fifties, European Catholicism was divided into those two camps.

Among the integralists were the Italian Jesuits, whom the Pope had invited to leave Rome in 1848, and to return in 1850. Their increased influence from that time on could be seen in the newspaper they founded, *La Civiltà Cattolica*, which became an important authoritarian and anti-liberal voice. In France, Louis Veuillot (1813–33), editor of the newspaper *L'Univers*, also won support among the clergy through his anti-liberalism campaign. To counteract their influence, Montalembert took over a monthly, *Le Correspondant*, and was soon joined by such liberal supporters as Monseigneur Dupanloup, outstanding bishop and preacher of Orleans.

Unfortunately, however, the movement to unify Italy hampered the cause of liberal Catholicism once again. Piedmont, a northern Italian state taken over by the liberals in 1848, became increasingly secularized under Prime Minister Camillo Cavour (1810–61). The Church lost control of education, its law courts were abolished, and most of its religious orders as well. All this the Pope saw as interference with the Church's

sovereignty over spiritual life. By 1858, however, the
Pope's temporal sovereignty was threatened as well.
Under the pretext of restoring order to uprisings he had
instigated, Cavour invaded the Papal States. In 1860 the
Pope's volunteer Catholic army lost to the well-trained
Piedmontese. And so, papal territory was reduced to a
narrow strip of land along the western coast of Italy,
known as the Patrimony of Saint Peter.

Montalembert and other Catholic liberals did not
endorse Cavour's activities. In fact, they considered his
actions a perversion of democracy and denounced him
as a plunderer. Despite their general advocacy of democracy, they felt that the Church-directed government
of the Papal States was necessary to ensure freedom
everywhere else. Nevertheless, the liberal Catholics
continued to press for the Church to be reconciled with
the modern ideals of freedom. At a congress held in
Malines in 1863 to get more widespread support for
liberal Catholicism, Montalembert argued that whatever their benefits, the old regimes uniting throne and
altar, and involving intolerance and Inquisitions were
dead, and the Church should welcome the new climate
of freedom. In fact, although the French Revolution had
been fought against the Church, its principals had
helped the Church grow more than the old regimes.
The French Church had prospered more under the liberal Louis Philippe than under the protection of the
Bourbons. The safeguard of democracy was Chris-
tianization, and Catholic and liberal Belgium proved
that the Church could flourish under a liberal regime.
These ideas were enthusiastically received by the Congress. Despite Montalembert's specific condemnation of
Cavour, however, Montalembert's ideas were too close

to those of Cavour and Lamennais for the Pope. His response was a friendly reminder to Montalembert of Pope Gregory's condemnation of those earlier views.

The quarrel between Catholic liberals and conservatives took different emphases in different countries. While the French and Italians were more concerned with external political freedom, German liberal Catholics were less interested in the relationship between the Church and the state. Their focus instead was on the issue of intellectual freedom within the Church. The political upheavals in France and Italy left Germany the center of Catholic intellectual activity. Because German theological schools were located in secular universities, the German liberals were keenly aware of the need for the Church to relate to modern culture and knowledge. They felt that the Church could effectively counter rationalist arguments only by adopting a similar scientific stance. Considering Scholasticism obsolete, they developed new scientific methods to defend the faith.

In reaction to rationalist denigration of the medieval Catholic tradition of Scholasticism, however, the Catholic conservatives endorsed a revival of Scholasticism. The nineteenth-century neo-Scholastic movement, like its sixteenth-century counterpart, was led by the Jesuits. In Italy these were associated with *La Civilità Cattolica*. In Germany, followers of Bishop von Ketteler (1811–77) mounted an aggressive campaign in the journal *Der Katholik*. They were supported by such influential clergy as Archbishop Reisach of Munich, Cardinal Rasucher of Vienna, and the Jesuit Kleutgen, considered the most original neo-Scholastic thinker in the nineteenth century.

By the middle of the nineteenth century, two fairly well-defined schools of thought had formed among German Catholics about the proper relationship of the Church to modern thought. The conservative Catholics, centered in Mainz, assumed a defensive posture. Seeing in modern culture only rationalism and secularism dangerous to the Church, they sought protection from contamination. To this end, they wanted priests trained in seminaries isolated from secular influence. They also wanted to strengthen Rome's authority over the Church. Thus they were called ultramontanes. In fact, they favored tight censorship by Rome for Catholic theologicans and scholars, not only in matters of dogma but in ordinary teaching as well. Since the Curia favored Scholasticism, this meant conformity to neo-Scholastic thought.

Ignaz von Doellinger (1799–1890), the leader of the German liberal Catholics centered in Munich, who opposed the ultramontanes, was originally both ultramontane and conservative. His historical studies of the Church, resulting in the four-volume *Church History* (1833–38) and *The Reformation* (1848), gradually led him to change to the liberal view. However, rather than seeing modern culture as a threat, he saw no reason that the Church should not be able to do as it had done in the past, adopting what was useful in the culture and avoiding what was not. In opposition to tight control from Rome, he felt it was extremely important for scholars and theologians to have greater intellectual independence. Doellinger's views were spread to England by his student Lord Acton (1834–1902). Together with the more moderate Catholic convert who became cardinal, John Henry Newman (1801–90), Acton promoted the cause of liberal Catholicism in the Catholic journal *The Rambler.*

Doellinger called a congress of German scholars that met in Munich in 1863, shortly after the congress of Malines. There Doellinger traced the history of the Church to show that Scholasticism was obsolete, and that the future of theology depended on knowledge of history and modern philosophy, disciplines most highly developed in Germany. He also made a plea for intellectual freedom for Catholic scholars. He argued that intervention by Church authorities should be necessary only in those rare cases when conclusions contradicted Church dogma. Lord Acton championed Doellinger's speech in his *Home and Foreign Review* for acknowledging and restricting Church authority to the area of dogma.

But Pope Pius was not pleased. In a private letter to Doellinger's archbishop, the Pope deplored Doellinger's attitude towards Scholasticism, and stated that Catholic scholars must be subject to the Church in ordinary teaching as well as in matters of dogma. Displeased because the congress had been held without asking permission from the Church hierarchy, the Pope saw Doellinger's speech as a challenge to Church authority. Faced with the congresses of Malines and Munich, together with his state of political siege, the Pope felt it was necessary to take action against liberalism. The result was his famous *Syllabus of Errors,* which appeared in 1864. That *Syllabus* was a summary of condemnations of modern errors that had been published in previous papal documents over the past fifteen years. These errors included rationalism, naturalism, socialism, and capitalism. Freedom of religion, progress, and liberalism were also condemned. The world had changed since the publication of *Mirari Vos*. In 1864 the statement that the Pope did not have to reconcile the Church with modern culture went against the grain of predominant thought. Public outcry arose at what seemed to be papal condemnation of a way of life that had been fought for and considered dearly won in England, France, Belgium, and North and Latin America.

The problem was that the publication of the *Syllabus* wrenched each denunciation out of its very specific context. In fact, the statement that the Church did not have to be reconciled with modern culture referred to the actions against the Church in Cavour's Piedmont. In its original context, the assertion was that if progress, liberalism, and modern culture meant anticlerical activity such as Cavour's, it was an error to think that the Church had to be reconciled with those things. Nevertheless, the way the condemnations appeared in the *Syllabus*, out of context, did seem to indicate that what began as condemnations of specific situations had been made into universal condemnations of the modern world.

Bishop Dupanloup (1802–78) made a heroic gesture to forestall misunderstanding by publishing a commentary on the *Syllabus* that put the condemnations back in their original contexts. He also tried to save the situation by making a distinction between thesis and hypothesis. Thus, he explained that the Church had denounced the thesis that it was universally ideal to have a society with competing religious beliefs, including ignorance of or hostility toward the Church. But it was wrong to infer from this thesis the hypothesis that the Church did not approve of having a broad measure of freedom of speech or the press in present society.

Many, however, considered Dupanloup's thinking specious. Although liberal Catholicism continued, the *Syllabus* achieved its effect. It put liberal Catholicism on the defensive, and silenced such campaigns as those of Montalembert and Lord Acton. On the other hand, the *Syllabus* was welcomed as part of a tendency towards centralization of authority in Rome by such ultramontanes as Veuillot, and Newman's fellow converts, William George Ward (1812–81) of the *Dublin Review*, and Henry Manning (1808–92), soon to be archbishop of Westminster.

Such centralization was in fact a by-product of the French Revolution, which had created many situations leading clergy and governments to deal directly with Rome. Clergy used to dealing with Rome when dioceses were left vacant continued to find protection in the power of the Pope against the whims of their state employers. Catholic minorities found the Pope especially useful in dealing with Protestant governments, while Protestant governments in turn preferred dealing with the Pope rather than with a strong national Church.

During his extremely long reign, Pope Pius encouraged and then promoted this centralization of papal authority. From the beginning he had tended to bypass the College of Cardinals, relying on such personal counselors as Giacomo Antonelli (1806–76), whom he made Secretary of State after his return from Gaeta. Shortly after that return, the Pope set an important precedent in his proclamation of the Immaculate Conception of the Virgin Mary, whose intercession he felt had aided his safe return. That proclamation established that the Pope could define dogma, consulting the Church only as he wished. In 1852 the Pope issued a proclamation to check Gallicanism in France. It prevented bishops from holding national councils that could become dangerous Gallican forums. Gallican books were placed on the Index. There was an increase in Roman liturgies, and clergy and laity were encouraged to appeal directly to Rome.

The Pope's personal style greatly aided strengthening papal authority. He gained control over the lower clergy by establishing such seminaries as the American College in Rome. In addition, he kept close personal contact with bishops, not hesitating to call them in to correct their views. In fact, the Pope's great popularity undoubtedly was related to his break with the tradition of papal isolation. He was the first modern Pope to use personal audiences extensively. And he enjoyed getting out and mingling with the people in Rome. In these ways he made personal devotion to the Pope part of modern Catholicism.

The question of papal authority became the issue when the Pope called the first Church council to meet in three hundred years. The Council of Trent had been called to define Catholic belief against the Protestant heresy. The First Vatican Council of 1869–70 was called to define the nature of the Church against the non-Christian philosophies that had undermined the very basis of Christian authority. The rejection of rationalism, naturalism, and pantheism, and the assertion of the unique, exclusive, and supernatural nature of Christian revelation were easily obtained. But the ultramontanes and the Pope felt that the position of a

Church in a liberal world could be further strengthened by affirming the *Syllabus of Errors* and defining the infallibility of the Pope. Although no one disputed the infallibility of papal pronouncements on dogma, the Gallicans and liberals opposed such a move as inopportune.

Some feared a popular tendency toward idolatry and the danger of attributing infallibility to any statement the Pope made. After the *Syllabus of Errors*, they feared centralization of authority in the hands of those who did not seem to understand the modern world. Doellinger and Dupanloup pointed out the dangers of trying to define an infallibility which had a murky historical basis. Maret pointed out that, historically, consent of the Church council was a requirement for the infallibility of papal pronouncements. The strong but minority opposition pointed out the danger of emphasizing an authoritarian Church in a world that prized freedom. Newman and others argued that it would hinder conversions. Many felt that such an assertion of the superiority of the Church over the state was unnecessary and politically unwise.

In the end, however, the Pope and the ultramontanes, who were in the vast majority, prevailed. The Vatican Council of 1870 settled the old quarrel between the council and the Pope in the Pope's favor by acknowledging the universal primacy of the Pope. The brilliant arguments of such minority leaders as Hefele, Rauscher, Ketteler, and Darboy were not entirely in vain, however. They won important modifications on the final statement of infallibility that the same Council passed. The statement referred to the Pope's doctrinal definitions, rather than simply the infallibility of the

Pope. Further qualifications stated the numerous conditions that needed to be met to make even those statements infallible.

The extension of papal spiritual authority did not come a minute too soon. That same week Napoleon III (1852–70) declared war on Prussia. The result was a withdrawal of French troops from Rome, and the occupation of the Patrimony of Saint Peter by the Piedmont army. The Pope considered himself a prisoner in the Vatican. In 1871 Rome became the capital of the new Italian state, marking the end of the oldest temporal sovereignty. The Papal States had often diverted papal attention from spirituality, and had long ceased to be a source of temporal power. But the Pope still felt strongly that the loss of that territory was a violation of the Church. For that reason he refused to acknowledge the new regime.

He refused to participate in the Law of Guarantees that would regulate the relationship between the papacy and the new state, and he refused compensation. The Law of Guarantees, however, acknowledged the Pope's special position as head of the worldwide Catholic Church. It allowed him his own postal, telegraphic, and diplomatic service, as well as his own personal guard. He was given exclusive use but not ownership of the Vatican, the Lateran, and the Castle Gandolfo. The state would not interfere with papal missives and directives. It would not nominate bishops, but they could not be invested without the consent of the state. From the Donation of Constantine to the permission of the Italian state, it was the end of an era.

VI

The Contemporary Church

The Missionary and American Church

THE VATICAN COUNCIL AFFIRMED A CHURCH THAT HAD rediscovered its sacramental nature. Its strongest counter to the cold, dry rationalism of the eighteenth century was a new piety that encouraged frequent reception of the sacraments and emphasized sentimental devotion, especially to the Virgin Mary. Pio Nono's strong and personal leadership was extremely influential in a renewal of inner spirituality in the Church. His long reign saw a sustained revival of religious orders.

Benedictine, Cistercian, and Carthusian monasteries showed new life. The Jesuits doubled their membership and the Dominicans and Franciscans prospered as well. Many new orders of men and women also sprang up. This renewed spirituality involved a continuation of the revival of mission activity begun by Pope Gregory XVI.

Under the leadership of Pope Pius IX, the Church that lost the Papal States in 1870 was once more embarked on becoming a worldwide Church. By the end of the reign of his successor, Pope Leo XIII (1848–1903), this status was solidly achieved. Pope Pius continued the missionary efforts that Pope Gregory had centered on the flourishing Catholic community of Goa in India. By the end of his reign many Jesuit colleges had been founded, and there were twenty bishops in India. The nineteenth-century revival of the Catholic mission in China saw 500,000 baptized Chinese Catholics, including 369 Chinese priests by 1891. Japan was closed to foreigners for two hundred years after its seventeenth-century massacre of Christians. Shortly after the Shogun reopened Japan to the world in 1854, Catholic missionaries were astonished to discover near Nagasaki approximately ten thousand Japanese who had secretly maintained their Christian faith in total isolation, without priests. Since Christianity was still outlawed in Japan, their discovery led to persecution and death. Pressure from the world press ended the persecution, however, and established complete freedom of worship in 1889. By 1891 a Japanese Church hierarchy was established with a metropolitan in Tokyo for 45,000 Catholics.

The revival of missionary activity in Africa was

spurred by the survival of David Livingstone's expedition in 1849. Hoping to make Algeria the base for conversion of the entire continent, the Archbishop of Algiers founded the Society of Missionaries of Africa, or "White Fathers," in 1868. After initial disasters, the mission gained a foothold in Uganda. Under the special protection of the Belgian government, however, the Belgian Congo mission had far greater success.

The greatest growth in Catholic missions during the nineteenth century, however, took place in North America. During the sixteenth and seventeenth centuries, the strongest Catholic posts were those the French Jesuits established in the Canadian lower Saint Lawrence valley. Thus began the predominantly French tradition that remains in the Canadian Roman Catholic Church today. By the 1830s the Catholic population in Montreal and Quebec was large enough to establish Quebec as the metropolitan. The predominantly French-Canadian exploration of the West created bishoprics at Winnipeg and Vancouver by 1860.

From Montreal and Quebec, French Jesuits also established such American missions as Detroit along the Great Lakes. Such Jesuits as Father Jacques Marquette (1637–75) explored the Mississippi and Ohio Valleys, establishing missions at St. Louis and Louisville, and ultimately reaching New Orleans. When the Jesuits were suppressed, their work was continued by such orders as the French Sulpicians, founded in 1642 and active during the French Revolution. In the Spanish territories of California, Florida and Texas the Franciscans established missions at such places as Los Angeles, San Francisco, St. Augustine and San Antonio.

In the thirteen American colonies the largest Catholic community was in Maryland, established as a haven from persecution for Christians in the seventeenth century. Outside the colonies a significant Catholic population was found in Pennsylvania, where the Quakers also established an atmosphere of religious toleration. The history of Catholicism in England after the sixteenth-century break with the Church, however, created an unfortunate fear that Catholicism necessarily involved both foreign interference and physical violence against Protestants. English anti-papal sentiment, which went at least as far back as the reign of Pope Innocent III, associated those fears with papal authority. Henry VIII's daughter, Mary Tudor (1553–58), restored Catholicism and papal authority to England against the will of the people. Her reign associated Catholicism with foreign intervention by her unpopular alliance with Catholic Spain despite nationalist objections. Fears of Spain's attempts to control England proved true when the Spanish Armada was launched to bring England back to Catholicism. Her reign also saw severe persecution of Protestants, associating Catholicism with Protestants being burned at the stake.

Queen Elizabeth I (1558–1603) ultimately made Catholicism synonymous with treason. At first the queen's compromise Church simply abolished papal authority and required an oath denying any foreign spiritual authority. After the Pope excommunicated the queen in 1570, however, it became treasonous to support the Pope in any way. By 1580 a secret French Jesuit mission to restore Catholicism in England led to the torture and hanging of Father Edmund Campion for plotting to overthrow the queen.

The association of Catholicism with tyranny and violence was reinforced in the seventeenth century by such actions as the spectacular Gunpowder Plot of 1605 to blow up the British parliament in retaliation for James I's (1603–25) reversal of his initial leniency toward Catholics. In 1672 the Catholic Charles II (1625–85) was forced to change his Declaration of Indulgence to include specific restrictions against Catholics in order to prevent a feared Popish plot to restore Catholicism. Increasing fear and suspicion of Catholicism throughout the 1670s allowed for the belief of Titus Oates's (1649–1705) fantastic tales of Jesuit invasions and Popish assassination plots. Finally, the uncircumspect Catholic James II (1685–88) was deposed for breaking his promises and the law in trying to impose Catholicism on England. In 1688 the Protestant William of Orange (1650–1702) and his wife Mary (1662–1694), daughter of James II, were invited from the Netherlands to share the English throne.

Unfortunately, settlers brought impressions of this history with them to America. Even in Maryland, when the Protestants quickly gained predominance they enacted repressive laws against Catholics to prevent the spread of Popery. And in 1774 the American Congress lost its chance for French-Canadian support of the Revolution with publication of its inflammatory letter, chastising Britain for recent recognition of Catholicism in Canada, and associating Catholicism with bigotry, persecution, murder, and rebellion. Perhaps the Congress saw the error of its ways as Catholic and Protestant Americans worked together to achieve independence. At any rate, the variety of religious denominations in different parts of the United States led to a policy of equal toleration for all religions, and so conditions improved for American Catholics after the Revolution of 1776.

The separation of church and state that was also built into the American Constitution undoubtedly facilitated the rapid development of the American Church. Without government interference, the Pope was free to appoint bishops, create dioceses, and establish colleges and seminaries when and where they were needed. In 1789 Rome appointed John Carroll (1735–1815) of Baltimore the first American bishop over a Catholic population of 35,000, out of four million Americans. With the help of such religious orders as the Carmelite, Poor Clare, and Visitation nuns, many convents and schools were established. The Sulpicians opened the first seminary in Baltimore. Elizabeth Seton founded the first native sisterhood, the Sisters of Charity, at Emmitsburg in Maryland in 1809. The Jesuits established Georgetown University. At Bishop Carroll's death in 1815, the Catholic American population had grown to nearly 200,000.

Interestingly enough, at the very time when Lamennais and the liberal Catholics were being condemned, the growth and survival of the young mission American Church as a free choice among competing religions provided evidence that Lamennais's ideas could work. Bishop Carroll's successor, the Irish John England (1786–1842), appointed bishop of Charleston, the Carolinas, and Georgia in 1820, even set up a short-lived experiment in democracy, allowing both clergy and laity to formulate the policy of each diocese. Bishop England was also influential in the formation of a series of Church councils held at Baltimore from 1829–1884.

By the fourth Baltimore Council the archiepiscopal see of Baltimore presided over fifteen other sees. Boston, New York, Philadelphia, and Bardstown (which became Louisville) were all established in 1808. Charleston and Richmond were established in 1820, Cincinnati in 1821, St. Louis and New Orleans in 1826. Detroit followed in 1833, Vincennes in 1834, Dubuque in 1837, and Nashville and Natchez in 1837.

The rapid expansion of the American Church from 1830 on was the result of massive immigration. In the first great wave, the large numbers of predominantly Irish immigrants increased the Catholic American population over 80 percent. Between 1830 and 1860 the Catholic population jumped from roughly 500,000 out of 12 million Americans to 3,103,000 out of 31.5 million. Unfortunately, such a massive and disproportionate change revived old fears. The result was an outbreak of violently anti-Catholic feeling that reached out from all along the eastern coast. During the thirties and forties the movement known as Nativism exploited old fears of Catholicism as foreign, superstitious, and idolatrous. Nativist "No-Popery" mobs lynched Catholics and burned their books, convents, and schools. The political situation in Europe in the 1850s increased anti-Catholic sentiment in the United States. The Pope's alliance with repressive governments against revolutions made him appear a tyrant to many Europeans and Americans.

Because the anti-Catholic movement took place at the same time as the development of the American schools, anti-Catholic feeling helped shape the unique character of the public schools. Initially, only Protestant religious instruction was given in the publicly funded schools, forcing other religions to build separate schools. Bishop John Hughes of New York (1797–1864) led the fight for public support for Catholic and Jewish schools as well. Bishop Hughes's plan was defeated, less on arguments of impracticality than on those of the immorality of using public funds to support Popery. The result was the elimination of all religious instruction in the public schools, and the establishment of a separate, private Catholic school system. By 1840 at least two hundred Catholic schools, half of them west of the Alleghenies, formed the basis of what became the largest system of private schools in the world. Recognition of the importance of the parochial school system in the growth and fostering of Catholicism is seen in the decree of the Baltimore Council of 1884 that every parish should have a school.

The growth of Catholicism in a Protestant and secular world was also fostered by a network of Catholic orphanages, hospitals, and old-age homes. Equally important was the formation of an American Catholic press. John England's highly influential *United States Catholic Miscellany*, founded in 1822, became a prototype for many other Catholic weeklies.

The American anti-Catholic movement cooled somewhat during the Civil War, and never regained its initial intensity. It continues to flare up from time to time, however. The American Protective Association was formed in the 1880s to help keep Catholics out of public office, and restrict their employment and possible influence in the work force. In the 1920s anti-Catholic feeling helped pass the Immigration Restriction Laws, and played a part in the activities of the Anti-Saloon

League. It was also a feature in the campaign against Al Smith, the first Catholic to run for the presidency.

Social Catholicism, Americanization and Modernization

The increase of the Catholic population of America was, of course, part of an unprecedented worldwide expansion of population. From the middle of the eighteenth century to the middle of the nineteenth, the population of Europe alone increased from 140 to 166 million. The increase in machines and technology associated with the Industrial Revolution which began in England and soon spread to continental Europe, brought masses to the cities again. The result was not only crowded living conditions but working situations that forced men, women, and children into long hours of tedious work at starvation wages. The growth of literacy and the popular press in the new mass society exposed workers to the way their problems were being addressed outside the Church. They were also becoming aware of the possibility of political power in emerging democracy.

Secular social theories attacked the capitalist economic system that allowed such a great disparity between prosperous owners and their oppressed workers. Liberals sought state intervention to ensure greater social equality. Socialism advocated collective ownership, which would allow workers to share in profits and receive social services. The democratic spirit of both philosophies pointed out the deficiencies of a Church that seemed to cling to old hierarchical values. Marxist theory went even further, declaring that religion had been used to keep workers oppressed, and indicating the necessity of class war and revolution. Because these theories seemed more responsive to the workers' needs than an outdated Church, by 1880, especially in France, the Church lost many workers to socialism.

In the mid-eighties, however, some Catholic voices had spoken out about the moral responsibility of the church to come to the aid of the workers. Bishop von Ketteler pointed out that it was the most serious problem of the times. His Catholic solution pointed out the dangers of socialism and liberal capitalism. He championed the rights of workers to form their own associations, and he called for a series of reforms including profit sharing, reasonable hours, rest days and regulation of female and child labor. In England, another theological conservative, Cardinal Manning, became the first English Roman Catholic bishop to promote the cause of the farmworkers in 1872. His ceaseless efforts on behalf of workers' rights and reform won him the respect which allowed his important role in settling the London dock strike of 1889. Cardinal Manning also helped reinforce the tendency already displayed by Pope Leo XIII to be more responsive to the changing times than was Pope Pius IX.

Especially in Europe, trade unions were often revolutionary and against the Church. But by the 1880s nonrevolutionary Christian trade unions run by the workers for their mutual protection and benefit were also being formed. In Europe these soon included the German Workers Welfare, the Belgian Anti-Socialist League, and the Belgian Democratic League. In America the largest labor union was the Knights of Labour, whose president, like most of its membership, was Catholic. Fear of revolution and violence had caused Canadian and American bishops to have its Canadian counterpart condemned, but the intervention of Cardinal Manning helped keep the Knights of Labour from a similar fate. Cardinal Gibbons of Baltimore (1877–1921) credited his success in averting the condemnation of Rome in 1886 to the advice Cardinal Manning gave to him and to the Pope as well.

The more responsive leadership of Pope Leo over that of Pope Pius could be seen in Pope Leo's different relationship with Otto von Bismarck (1815–98). The Iron Chancellor of Germany waged a Kulturkamp against the Church involving repressive acts similar to those of Cavour. With the death of Pope Pius, however, Bismarck's and his attitude changed, and Pope Leo's untiring energy achieved a dissolution of the alliance of the liberals and Bismarck against the German Catholic Party and the Church. By 1888 the new German Emperor, William II (1888–1918), acknowledging the Pope's concern for workers, asked him to cooperate in his conference on workers' benefits. Once again, the Pope's cordial response had received great encouragement from Cardinal Manning.

The *Rerum Novarum* issued in 1891 by Pope Leo XIII then gave authoritative expression to a concern for the very real social problems faced by the Church in an industrial age. This document, often called the Magna Carta of social Catholicism, became the basis for Catholic teaching on social justice in modern times. It directed the Church to face modern social problems squarely. Through it, Pope Leo criticized the socialist solution and endorsed the capitalist system of private property, but he also affirmed as Catholic tradition the denunciation of exploitation and excessive profit. He championed the human dignity of workers, together with their right to organize to achieve better conditions. What is more, the *Rerum Novarum* directed the Church to play an active role in the struggle to eliminate social injustice and inequality.

Rome's endorsement of social Catholicism was necessary in part to dissociate social reform from the more suspect theology of some of its liberal advocates. This was the case in America, for example, where suspicion of its supporters was involved in the request to condemn the Knights of Labor. By the 1880s the second wave of immigration made the American Catholic population predominantly German, rather than Irish. The Germans and Irish had different ideas about the best way to preserve the faith in the new world. Basically, such German leaders as Archbishop Corrigan of New York and Bishop McQuaid of Rochester were conservative and separatist. On the other hand, such Irish leaders as Archbishop John Ireland of St. Paul (1830–1918) and Bishop John Keane, rector of the new Catholic University of America, were liberal progressives who wanted to blend Catholicism into American culture.

The Germans were concerned to preserve their German heritage in the midst of an established Irish-American hierarchy. They claimed that when Germans were placed under Irish bishops and priests, the difference in custom and language made many leave the faith. Consequently, they requested German-trained bishops. They particularly outraged the Irish when a European layman, Peter Paul Cahensly, intervened with the Pope to request separate ethnic parishes in America to rectify this situation. Afraid of being absorbed by other religions as well as by other cultures, the Germans also vehemently denounced the public school system and insisted on separate Catholic schools.

In contrast, the Irish sought to minimize differences with other cultures. No doubt influenced by the anti-Catholic movement, they argued that removing the foreign image of the Church would stimulate more conversion. Their movement, known as Americanization, sought to adapt Catholic traditions to the modern spirit of cooperation, democracy, and social reform at the heart of their vision of America. They hoped that Catholic University, which opened in 1899, would train American clergy imbued with this new spirit. The Irish also sought cooperation with the public schools. The Germans were particularly incensed by John Ireland's proposal to make Catholic schools public during the day, with religious instruction after hours. Additionally, the Irish urged that, if necessary, Catholics should join non-Catholic organizations aimed at social reform. The peak of Irish cooperative ventures came with their participation in the Chicago Parliament of Religions in 1893, where representatives of worldwide religions publicly and jointly declared their belief in basic religious truths.

Although the Irish Americans were firm Catholics, completely loyal to Rome, the Germans saw much of their behavior as a dilution of Catholic faith. And, indeed, their activities verged on dangerous ground. For example, many organizations for social reform were secret societies like the Freemasons. And the anti-clerical tendency of that organization caused Pope Clement XII to prohibit Catholics from joining it in 1738, a prohibition which is still in effect today. Also, since for German Catholics the history of the reformation was still felt, agreement with non-Catholics was dangerously close to denying the unique character of Catholicism. Such a state of mind was condemned as the heresy of indifferentism in the *Syllabus of Errors*. In fact, the German and Jesuit theologians accused the Irish of disloyalty to the Church, indifferentism, and the false liberalism which the *Syllabus* also condemned. The German attacks mounted both through public speeches and a journalistic campaign in the *American Ecclesiastical Review* and *Civilta Cattolica*.

The Pope interfered very little in the activities of the American Church, which as a missionary Church remained under the direction of the Mission for the Propagation of the Faith until 1908. In line with his general policy of reconciliation, he sided with the voices of moderation, urging the cessation of sharp attacks. When it was clear, however, that the American Church was on the verge of a split, the Pope intervened. In 1892 he sent Monsignor Francesco Satolli as the first representative of Rome to the American Church to heal the split. Satolli at first sided with John Ireland and the liberals, but then changed his views and was instrumental in the removal of the progressive Monsignor O'Connell as rector of the American College in Rome in 1895, and of Bishop Keane from Catholic University the following year.

Meanwhile the American quarrel was also brought to Europe. In 1892 John Ireland generated great interest in his ideas by his effective speeches in France. In that country liberals were mindful of the way the American Church was carrying out the program advocated by Lamennais, and touted that experiment as proof of the possibilities of democracy and separation of Church and state. Interest turned to enthusiasm, however, with the publication of a French translation of an American biography of a leading influence on the American Irish, Father Isaac Hecker. A convert to Catholicism, Father Hecker founded the order known as the Paulists, who promoted his ideas about the necessity of adapting the Church to the American spirit in their journal, *The Catholic World*. A preface to the French translation by John Ireland praised Father Hecker for showing the entire Church how to adapt to the modern world.

What was possible in the United States, which was founded on the principles of democracy, toleration, and separation of church and state, however, was not equally possible in the different situations of Europe, and especially post-Revolutionary France. There the ideas of rationalism and naturalism continued to be popular. The Pope had allowed the Chicago Parliament of Religions, but in France, where one tended to be either a Catholic or a nonbeliever, the Church hierarchy did not allow a similar demonstration at the Paris World Exhibition the following year. The dangers of Montalembert and Doellinger were still fresh. Soon, the ultramontanes, together with royalists, members of religious orders, and others as well, mounted a vigorous attack against the ideas known as Americanism.

In the end, Pope Leo himself saw the dangers of a

threat to the integrity of the Church, and sided with those who saw a violation of the authoritarian spirit established by the Vatican Council and the Syllabus of Errors. In 1899 he wrote a letter to Cardinal Gibbons and, stating that it was more necessary for France than America, condemned Americanism if it promoted the following false ideas: the necessity of the Church to adapt to modern ideas of freedom and authority; the greater importance of such natural active virtues as honesty and temperance over passive supernatural virtues; the greater value of an active, external spirituality over the interior, passive spirituality of the many enclosed religious orders; and the greater necessity of guidance from the internal voice of the Holy Spirit than from any external source. Ireland and his followers claimed that their ideas did not promote these errors and accepted the Pope's judgment. The fight between the Germans and the Irish calmed down and the American Church fell into line with the authoritarianism of Europe.

Pope Leo XIII was much more interested in the intellectual life of the Church than Pio Nono had been. He opened the secret Vatican archives to all scholars and set up a Biblical Commission to update the study of the Bible. But like Pope Pius, he was not a liberal. His endorsement of social reform, his support of the French Republic, and his ultimate stand against Americanism all came from his firm faith in the conservative theology of Scholasticism and Thomas Aquinas. In 1879 Pope Leo declared Thomism the official Catholic philosophy. He also required its study and founded an institute for that purpose at Louvain in Belgium.

The later nineteenth century, however, was the

period when Darwin's evolutionary view of the development of human life increased the influence and popularity of such materialistic philosophies as Marxism. It was also a period of enormous strides in historical criticism of the Bible and the origins of Christianity. These developments especially made many Catholic scholars increasingly dissatisfied with the general ignorance of historical methods of the leading neo-Thomist scholarship. They felt that Thomism was simply time-bound, and could not adequately deal with the different problems the Church had to face in modern times. Thus, the attitude that came to be known as Modernism raised the question recurring from Erasmus through Acton—of adapting Catholic theology to modern time.

The two most controversial Modernist thinkers were the French priest Alfred Loisy (1857–1940) and the English Jesuit George Tyrrell (1861–1909). Loisy's historical research into the creation of the Bible challenged the authority of Church tradition. He lost his chair at the Institut Catholique in Paris in 1893 for his assertions that discrepancies between the Bible and historical and scientific facts revealed that Moses could not have written the Pentateuch. Undaunted, Loisy continued with his work, publishing his explosive book *L'Evangile et l'Eglise* in 1903. In that work Loisy emphasized Jesus as a historical man rather than as being both human and divine. He claimed that Jesus' mission was to prophesy that the end of the world was near at hand. He also argued that the Church, Roman primacy, and the sacraments arose only through historical necessity when that predicted end failed to arrive. The teachings of the Church are therefore not fixed and unchanging, but an account of its historical experience. The obvious denial of the divinity of Christ and the origins of the Church created an uproar. The book and other of Loisy's writings were condemned and placed on the Index.

Tyrrell, a convert with a strong mystical leaning, was concerned to emphasize the interior quality of faith which he felt was lost in the dry intellectual abstractions of Scholastic teaching. He stressed dogmatic formulations as intellectual interpretations of an essentially inspired imaginative revelation, and pointed out that such dogmatic expressions must necessarily change through time. Although Tyrrell was accused of reverting to Protestantism, he considered himself a Catholic because of his strong belief in the community of the faithful that constitutes the Church, and especially the idea that it is the Church that enables a relationship with the divine. Nevertheless, he was opposed to the authoritarianism of the Church, and wanted a democratic Church with officials who would represent the evolving consensus of the community.

Pope Pius X, however, continued Pope Leo's affirmation of the authoritarian Church. He was not concerned to adapt the Church to the modern world. Undoubtedly this resolve was only strengthened by the traumatic separation of church and state in France in 1905, the end of a long anticlerical campaign. In 1906 the Biblical Commission declared that all Catholics must consider Moses the author of the Pentateuch. In 1906 the Pope issued the decree *Lamentabili*, which catalogued errors related to the interpretation of the Bible and Church teaching. The decree insisted on the truth and historical accuracy of the Bible, the sacraments, and the primacy of Rome. It asserted that Church dogma might develop, but it could not substantially change. The *Pascendi* decree, which followed shortly after, collected most of the ideas found in the works of Loisy, Tyrrell, and others and condemned them as the false thinking of Modernism. The decree condemned the general Modernist tendency to emphasize the intuitional, subjective, and mystical aspect of faith over the rational, and reaffirmed the objective, supernatural, and external character of Catholic faith. It saw the root of the Modernist error in the concept of Immanentism, the assertion that religious experience begins with an awareness of an inner religious need, and the corollary, that the sacraments objectify this inner need. It also condemned agnosticism, the idea that nothing can be known beyond the senses.

The excessively sharp tone of the language of condemnation reveals how much the ideas associated with Modernism threatened the very basis of the belief and structure of the Post-Trent Church. Pope Pius felt that the danger exceeded even that of Protestantism and rationalism because the ideas undermined the foundation of the Church from within. In order to wipe out the heresy, a vigilance committee was set up in every diocese, with a group of censors to inspect all literature. The strict secrecy of the proceedings was reminiscent of the medieval Inquisitions. In addition, seminaries were to be instructed that Scholasticism and Thomism are the basis of all sacred studies, and the clergy were to take an oath against Modernism.

The measures proved effective. Tyrrell denounced the condemnation in the *London Times*. He, Loisy, and others were excommunicated. Modernism was stamped out. But there was a price. Many of the brightest scholars left the Church. Repression ruled the seminaries. Rome became known for its intellectual sterility. And the questions were raised again later in the twentieth century.

VII

The Twentieth-Century Church

BEFORE THE MODERNIST QUESTION WAS RAISED AGAIN, however, the twentieth-century Church faced the problems of increasing secularism and two World Wars. The reign of Pope Pius's successor, Pope Benedict XV (1914–22), was devoted to encouraging peace, reconciliation, and relief for victims of war. Within the Church he stopped many of the activities that had resulted in a witchhunt for Modernists. He restored diplomatic relations with the French state, and relaxed conditions in Italy so that Catholics could participate in the Christian Democratic party. Pope Benedict helped offset losses to secularism in Catholic Europe by his revolutionary missionary decree which called for the end of nationalistic attitudes together with respect for native cultures and promotion of native clergy. Despite these measures, however, Pope Benedict's reign revealed a decline in papal prestige. His determination to remain neutral in 1917, condemning all war as unjust, rather than taking sides, caused his call for peace to be ignored. He was excluded from the peace conference in 1919 that resulted in the Treaty of Versailles, ending World War I.

The strength and authority of the papacy were quickly restored by Pope Benedict's successor, Pope Pius XI (1922–39). For the first time since 1846, he gave the papal blessing from the Vatican, signaling restored peace with postwar Italy. He also revived direct papal action. Like Pope Pius VII, the new Pius secured the rights of the Church through a series of Concordats negotiated with the dictators who came to power during his reign. In Italy, the Pope saw Mussolini's Fascism, committed to upholding law, order, private property, and Christian morality as a lesser danger than Communism, committed to overthrowing the hierarchy to install a classless, atheistic state. Consequently, the Pope transferred support from the Catholic political party whose pacifism had not checked the Communist offensive, to the Fascists whose action defeated it. Although Mussolini was also an atheist, like Napoleon he saw an advantage in accommodating the Church in a predominantly Catholic country. The result was the Lateran Treaty of 1929, which provided financial compensation for the loss of the Papal States and awarded the Pope complete sovereignty over the forty-acre complex of buildings and grounds around St. Peter's in Rome, known as the Vatican. The treaty also acknowledged Catholicism as the official religion to be taught in the schools, and protected religious orders and processions. Fascism itself, however, soon took on the trappings of a religion, and the struggle between the Pope and Mussolini, especially for control over youth activities, made Fascism and Catholicism increasingly incompatible. In 1926 the Pope condemned the Fascist French Action Française of Charles Maurras.

In Germany the support of the Pope and the Catholic Center Party for Hitler won the Church the Concordat of 1933. Its terms, however, like those of an agreement with Fascist Spain in 1935, were never upheld. In 1937 the Pope's stinging condemnation of Nazism, *Mit Brennender Sorge,* smuggled into Germany and read from the pulpits, resulted in severe retaliation against the Church.

In 1931 Pope Pius also reaffirmed the principles of social Catholicism, publishing his *Quadragesimo Anno* to mark the fortieth anniversary of the *Rerum Novarum.* In the midst of the economic depression between the two World Wars, the Pope updated his support of capitalism, seeking greater protection for workers against a totalitarian state, and warning against the dangers now of Communism rather than socialism. The Pope also organized the Catholic Action League, a lay movement to provide spiritual direction and influence public policy with Catholic values.

This policy helped foster the increasing coalition between workers' movements and the Catholic Church in such countries as the United States. There the Church hierarchy had become involved in social action when the National Catholic War Council was founded to coordinate Catholic contributions to the war effort during the First World War. After the war, the National Catholic Welfare Conference was set up as a permanent peacetime coordination agency for Catholic affairs. Under the vigorous direction of the priest John A. Ryan

(d. 1945), its department of social action issued a Bishops' Program calling for legislation to guarantee the workers' rights to collective bargaining, minimum wages, social security, and health and unemployment insurance. Despite initial resistance, ultimately much of this program was incorporated into New Deal policy.

Ryan's call to the social conscience of Catholic laity was met with the Catholic Worker movement founded in 1933 by the Catholic convert Dorothy Day and Peter Maurin, who identified with the poor, homeless, and unemployed. Their House of Hospitality, which provided food, comfort, and shelter in New York's Bowery, attracted many young Catholics dedicated to living a life that would put Church teaching on social justice into action. Setting up similar houses throughout the States, they combined their devotion to prayer and the sacraments with voluntary poverty, living the life of the poor among the poor. Their lives were an example of the personal responsibility for social injustice that they stressed, and a living protest against the impersonal character of a mechanistic society. They established a paper, *The Catholic Worker*, which soon reached a circulation of a hundred thousand. Dedicated to the cause of labor, the Movement fearlessly attacked such problems in the American system as materialism, racism, and imperialism, and espoused nonviolence and pacifism. After the formation of the CIO in America in 1935, many priests took an active role in workers' lives, as well as in working to instruct labor leaders in Catholic social doctrine.

In 1939, shortly after the coronation of Pope Pius XII (1939–58), Hitler plunged the world into World War II. Poised between the double dangers to the Church from

Nazism and Communist Russia, the new Pope assumed a public posture of neutrality. Behind the scenes, however, he worked to ensure that neither one was completely victorious. The Pope refused to give support to the Nazi rhetoric, which gave anti-Communism as a pretext for invasion. On the other hand, the Pope was equally unwilling to voice public condemnation of the horrendous crimes he knew the Nazis were committing against not only Jews and Poles, but all humanity. Papal silence is often justified on the basis of the undeniably great complexity of the situation. The private help that made the Vatican give refuge to five thousand Jews is seen as more prudent than the possibly worse recriminations which public exposure might have caused. Moreover, the Church was not alone in its silence. Nevertheless, the lost chance to provide the world with a firm moral public stand clouds the reign of Pope Pius XII.

With the end of the war came a shift in political power. The Western powers of the United States and its ally Great Britain stood poised against the power of the Communist Soviet Union in the East. Communist denial of the basic truths of Christianity and supernatural religions became the most severe threat to the Church since eighteenth-century rationalism. The end of the war saw the Soviet Iron Curtain close round the Churches in Eastern Europe, cutting off relationships with Rome. As more and more countries were overrun, and Churches in Poland, Czechoslovakia, Hungary, Yugoslavia, and the Baltic States oppressed, the Vatican became increasingly vocal in its alliance with Western powers. In contrast to his neutrality during the war, Pope Pius XII used every effort, including broadcasts by Vatican radio, to mobilize world opinion against the Communists. The growth of the Communist parties in France and Italy put Italy and Rome under genuine danger of a Communist takeover. In the face of this threat, in 1949 the Pope issued a carefully worded decree, automatically excommunicating all Catholics who consciously and freely joined the international Communist party. The Vatican's efforts against Communism were supported by such prominent Catholic statesmen of the Christian Democratic Alliance as West German Chancellor Konrad Adenauer (1876–1967), French Premier Robert Schuman (1886–1963), and Italian Premier Alcide De Gasperi (1881–1967), a former Vatican librarian.

By the fifties, the papacy was at the peak of its prestige. Many dignitaries came to Rome to confer with the Pope. Millions of humble worshipers came to Rome on a pilgrimage for the Holy Year of 1950. Most nations, including the United States, had permanent representatives at Rome. The Pope gave daily addresses on many subjects and was quoted around the world. The Pope's authoritarian attitude could be seen in the assertion of papal infallibility of his decree on the bodily assumption of Mary that year. But he also created a non-Italian majority in the College of Cardinals for the first time. The Church had seen a steady growth in foreign missions creating a network of Roman Catholic churches, universities, schools, orphanages, and homes for the aged throughout Asia, Africa, and India. Uganda had 150,000 converts by World War I. In China, despite the strong anti-Christian campaign of militant Communists under Mao Tse-tung, there were three million Catholics by 1937. In Japan the number of Catholics increased from 108,000 in 1936 to 121,000 by World War II. The population of Catholics in East Africa reached 2.5 million by 1949.

The growth in Catholic population led to increased native hierarchies in each case. During the postwar boom the Catholic population continued its expansion. The number of Catholic dioceses increased from 1,696 to 2,048 during the Pope's reign. The fifties saw rapid growth in the Catholic population of such Asian countries as Korea. By 1959 thirty-six percent of the Belgian Congo were Catholic, and by 1962 there were six million Catholics in India. A bank, or Institute for the Works of Religion, was established to manage the boost to the Vatican's economy created by this postwar growth. The sense of the way the Church had become established in the United States could be seen from the growth of the American Catholic population to reach 20.9 percent by 1958 and from the election of John F. Kennedy in 1960 as the first Catholic president of the United States.

Without doubt, however, the outstanding event of the twentieth-century Church was the election of Pope John XXIII (1958–63). The period of the late fifties saw an entire world coming to a new awareness of the great changes that had taken place in the period between the two World Wars and the Cold War between the West and the Communist block that dominated the fifties. Of course, these scientific, technological, social, and cultural developments had been taking place over a considerable period of time, but only toward the end of the relative peace and stability of the fifties was their impact being felt. New explorations in space, together with increased use of cars, planes, telephones, telegraphs, radios, movies, and T.V. created a smaller and more connected world than that of which people had been conditioned to think. There was a new sense that the world needed to be viewed more as a global village than separate nation states. The sense that things were going beyond what they had been was being conveyed by the new term for the times, the "postmodern" age.

New times require new ways. Elected as a compromise between traditional and more progressive candidates, the new Pope surprised many who expected an interim Pope who would bide his time. Instead, during his brief reign, Pope John revolutionized the Church, bringing an end to the Tridentine era. Those who were surprised, however, would have done well to consider his actions throughout his clerical career. From the time he entered the seminary at his beloved Bergamo as a youth of eleven in 1892, the Pope found himself in a Church that was forced to deal with an increasingly secularized world.

In that northern town the youth saw his bishop counter the hostility of the Italian government to the Church and the possible attractions of materialistic Marxism by encouraging the formation of the Catholic workers' associations which ultimately became the Catholic Action League. After his ordination in 1904, the young priest learned even more as secretary to his beloved mentor Bishop Radini-Tedeschi, who, among other things, used his own money to support a strikers' fund. The young priest's quick application of the lessons he had learned in not only adapting to a hostile environment, but also in countering its effects can be seen in his use of his military career. Not only did he earn friends among the anticlerical military when he was drafted into the army at the beginning of World War I, but he used his small military pay at the end of the war to establish a Catholic Student House to counter the attempts of both the Communists and the Fascists to attract postwar youth.

As papal representative to Bulgaria, Turkey, and Greece, after being made archbishop in 1925, the Pope found himself among governments that were often politically unstable and antireligious. In addition, he faced the wariness and rivalry of leaders of the predominant schismatic Orthodox Church, who feared coercion to rejoin the Roman Catholic Church. Even among those who still acknowledged the primacy of the Latin Church, there were those who followed Orthodox Byzantine rather than Latin rites. Pope John, however, managed to turn these difficult situations into opportunities to create bridges between the Church and its antagonists. He showed respect for those who disagreed with the Church by quietly obeying even anticlerical laws, going out of his way to establish contact with them. And so he created a dialogue and won over even those government leaders who at first barely acknowledged or tolerated his presence.

Within the Church community as well, he respected the jurisdiction of the Orthodox leaders and went out of his way to establish dialogues that might help heal divisions at some future time. His concern to make connections between the Eastern and Western Church led him to use his stay in Turkey to produce a history of the Oriental Church. The same concern increased his pleasure at his appointment as Patriarch of Venice, a city which he viewed as a bridge between East and West.

Wherever the Pope went, his presence made a difference. Throughout his clerical career he not only worked hard to transform the idea of a remote hierarchy into one that was available and accessible, but also went out to meet its people. Never forgetting his peasant origins or his pastoral concerns, at each post he endured physical hardships in order to visit as many simple parishes as he could. He did his best to involve the simplest people in the life of the Church, including requesting the removal of marble panels at the Basilica of San Marco because they were depriving the worshipers of seeing and hearing the celebration of Mass.

This simple and unpretentious man did not greatly change his ways when he became Pope. The man who had written about history and taken pains to restore many buildings wherever he had been, respected tradition. But he also quietly introduced change. Believing that a gloomy priest does not fully express the right appreciation of God's works, Pope John embraced the modern world as part of God's creation. The man who, as Patriarch of Venice, had been happy to fly to Lourdes on a modern jet to celebrate the hundredth anniversary of the vision of the Virgin Mary, and to bless the basilica from an open convertible, became the first Pope to leave the sanctuary of Rome. Always eager to use modern inventions to reach the people, he became the first Pope in nearly a hundred years to travel by train. On that journey through Italy, thousands of worshipers viewed their Pope for the first time. Embracing modern culture to further God's work, the man who broke precedent by inviting the modern composer Stravinsky to conduct his oratorio in the Great Basilica of San Marco, became the first Pope to visit the theater in two hundred years when he saw and enjoyed a performance of T.S. Eliot's *Murder in the Cathedral.*

Above all, the Pope won the hearts of the people by his unabashed love of life and *all* of humanity, which his encylical *Pacem in Terris* addressed for the first time. He restored the sense of the Pope as a human being. Although he had revived the custom of receiving papal audiences in the Vatican, he could not have enough contact with the people. He threw Vatican security into a tizzy by his propensity for visiting hospitals and prisons, and simply mingling with people in the street on his own. And he delighted all by his ability to make jokes, especially about himself.

And so Pope John proved a new kind of Pope who was exactly right for the times. The first indication of the changes he would make was his choice of the name Pope John, a name avoided because of its last use by the notorious anti-Pope John at the time of the Council of Constance. Restoring the sense of "good news" originally associated with the name John, the new Pope John XXIII made his most important change. Reviving the best of the spirit of the Council of Constance, Pope John called for an ecumenical council to promote the unity of all Christian peoples. And so the new Pope summoned the historical Second Vatican Council, the first Council to meet in over ninety years.

Meeting in four sessions from 1962–65, this Council at last brought the Church in line with changing times. The makeup of this Second Vatican Council indicated some of the changes that had occurred since the First Vatican Council. Not only were there 3,000 in attendance as compared with the 737 of Vatican I, but this twenty-first Council was also more truly "ecumenical" or worldwide in its representation. While the earlier Council had been dominated by European representatives, now there were roughly a thousand from Europe, slightly less than that from North and South America, together with smaller delegations from Asia, Africa, Central America, and Oceania—and many of these were native clergy from the mission Churches. There were a greater number of non-Catholics and laity than ever before, as well as representatives from almost every other major Christian Church. All were truly welcomed as family, and no other Council had received worldwide coverage through newspapers, radio, and television.

Most important of all, however, was the tone that Pope John established of a heart-to-heart dialogue with all of humanity on the major spiritual issues of the day. In his opening address, Pope John dissociated himself from the reactionary and defensive posture of the Tridentine Church. He proposed a policy of optimism, faith, and charity toward the modern world, rather than negation and condemnation. He warned that what was needed was not sterile discussion of doctrine, but new and fresh ways of bringing the Catholic faith to the modern world in terms that it could understand and use. In part, those warnings were directed to the Curia, which was dominated by cardinals who feared the winds of change they felt in the air. They controlled preparation of the agenda and proposals to be before the Council, and their documents were loaded with conservative language, which they clearly hoped would be rubber-stamped. They had also already handpicked the names of conservative delegates they hoped to have quickly elected to the ten key committees that would control the substance of the debates. Their plan fell through, however, when the bishops demanded time to draw up their own lists. As a result, the men who were elected tended to be independent and representative of the worldwide Church. The first session saw genuine dialogue between the conservative faction led by the Italian delegation and half of the American delegations, and the progressive faction, led by the West German, French, Belgian, Dutch, Spanish, and other half of the American delegations. It was agreed that Vatican II would become the Council on the Church, as Vatican I had been the Council on the Pope. The focus would be both on the meaning of the Church to those within it and on its relationship to the world outside.

The world was shocked and dismayed when Pope John died in 1963 before the next session could begin. But fears that Pope John's work might die with him were allayed with the election of Pope Paul VI (1963–78), the bookish Archbishop of Milan, whose father had been a prominent Italian journalist. The new Pope, whom Pope John had honored by making First Cardinal and reputedly hoped would be chosen his successor, proved committed to Pope John's goals.

When he reconvened the Council in 1963 he immediately continued it on the path Pope John had begun, rededicating it to the spirit of renewal, reunion, and dialogue with the world. At its conclusion the council had produced sixteen documents. All were almost unanimously approved, and most enacted changes which would radically transform the contemporary Church. The change that was undoubtedly most immediately felt by all was the decision to translate the liturgy from traditional Latin into the native language of each Church. The document on the liturgy, which was debated while Pope John was still alive, also advised making sure that the laity could understand the liturgy. It encouraged lay participation in every way as well.

The document *Lumen Gentium* also transformed the attitude toward the structure of the Church. The old emphasis on rigid separation between an authoritative clergy and an obedient laity was shifted to an emphasis on the whole Church as the people of God and on the common priesthood of the clergy. The emphasis on an authoritative and isolated Pope was replaced by the emphasis on collegiality, the participation of the bishops as a whole in the Pope's authority over the Church.

What was equally startling to many traditional Catholics was an entirely new attitude toward the non-Catholic world, an attitude which can be largely attributed to the leadership of both Pope John and Pope Paul. The document *Unitatis Redintegratio* changed the goal of returning Protestants to the Church to one of the ultimate reunion of all Christians. Although the Church still maintained its unique status as a means of complete salvation, it stressed its unity with other Christians. Acknowledging them as true ecclesial communities, the Church urged its members to work toward ultimate unity by entering into a dialogue of talk, prayer, and social action with them. It also admitted its own part in creating and perpetuating disunity among Christians and committed itself to continual reformation to eliminate the error. The Council did not limit its concern to the Christian community. It passed a con-

demnation of anti-Semitism. And Pope Paul's historic
visit to the United Nations to appeal for peace in 1965
made graphic the Council's statement on the right to
freedom in religious practice and belief. This spirit of
concern for all humanity was also perceived and conveyed by the enthusiastic reception of Pope Paul's pilgrimage to the Eucharistic Congress in Bombay.

Finally, the Council endorsed an entirely new recep-
tive attitude towards history. The use of historical criticism in research on the Bible and the Church, which
had been problematic since at least the Renaissance,
was finally accepted. Recognition that historical con-
ditioning affected all aspects of the Church and its
sacred books replaced the old insistence on non-
historical Scholasticism. Acknowledgment of a complex development of liturgical forms, customs, and
dogma through history replaced an insistence on apostolic origins. For the first time in modern history the
document On the Church in the Modern World expressed an acceptance of changing forms of thought
and feeling and an acknowledgment of the possibilities
for human liberation in the progressive cultural and
social developments of contemporary life.

Pope Paul not only saw that the reforms envisioned
by Pope John were passed by the Vatican Council but
before that Council was over, the Pope had already
begun to see that Pope John's visions were instituted in
other ways. Utilizing the vast experience of his thirty-
two years of service with the Vatican Secretariat of
State, Pope Paul extended Pope John's sense of leadership by bringing the Church to the people on an
international scale. While Pope John was the first Pope
to leave the Vatican in many years, Pope Paul's historic

trips to Jerusalem and Bombay in 1964 made him the first Pope to leave Italy in one hundred and fifty years. The following year he interrupted his leadership at the Vatican Council and dramatized the leadership the Church could provide the world, utilizing the modern miracle of the jet, by personally appearing to ratify the United Nations in New York. In 1969 Pope Paul became the first Pope ever to visit Africa and, in 1970, Southeast Asia. He had spent some time in Warsaw as part of the Vatican diplomatic staff, and is credited with opening up relationships between the Vatican and Communist countries. Under his rule, leaders of the Communist countries visited the Vatican for the first time.

Before the Council was over, Pope Paul had also begun to institute Pope John's vision of ecumenism. Up until this time that movement had been mainly Protestant, beginning with the World Missionary Conference in Edinburgh in 1910. Pope Paul's visit to the headquarters of the World Council of Churches at Geneva in 1971, where he recited the Lord's Prayer with world church leaders, became symbolic of the changes he was helping to create. In 1967 the Pope's meeting with the Orthodox Patriarch Athenagoras was the first meeting between heads of the Roman and Eastern Church since 1439. Historically, the areas of disagreement between the Church and the Orthodox and Protestant Churches have included papal primacy, infallibility, the relationship between Scriptures and tradition, the minister, and the meaning of the Eucharist and the significance of Mary. By 1968 and 1970 a Lutheran-Catholic Consultation had come to see agreement about the sacrificial nature of the Eucharist and the presence of Christ in that sacrament. Talks between Anglicans and

Catholics had begun in 1966, and by 1971 similar agreement had been reached on the nature of the Eucharist. By 1974 Catholics and American Lutherans came to some agreement about the historicity and need for the office of the Bishop of Rome for Christian unity. The Lutherans, however, felt that before they could accept any such papal primacy the autocratic and bureaucratic features of the office would have to be changed. Similarly, by 1975 Anglicans also agreed on the value of the universal primacy of office of Bishop of Rome, but indicated that before they could accept the primacy of such an office for themselves their reservations about the abuse of papal power and two Marian dogmas would have to be overcome.

Within the Church, Pope Paul provided similar strong leadership. Before the Council was over he helped institute collegiality by setting up an international Bishops Synod, to continue the work of the Council. The representative body would meet every two years in Rome to set up similar councils of priests in their own dioceses. In addition, the Pope helped see that such reforms as the vernacular Mass, easing restrictions about fasting and even intermarriage were carried out. Within a few short years, however, the Second Vatican Council had recommended changes the church had been resisting for four hundred years. Moreover, during the late sixties when these changes were endorsed, revolutions and student riots were challenging the foundations of the Judeo-Christian heritage and political and social institutions throughout the world. The legacy of Vatican II became the problem of dealing with a changing Church in a rapidly changing world. For the average member of the Church this problem was symbolized by the transformation of the Church service after Vatican II. For many, the traditional Latin prayers and strict separation between clergy and congregation were comfortable and known. They had been brought up to watch the priest's back while he whispered prayers in Latin. When the service was changed so that the priest now faced them and spoke in a language they could understand, they were disoriented and confused. Such changes represented a loss of the familiar in a world that seemed too eager to change and discard what was known. These members felt uncomfortable, distressed, and even betrayed.

On the other hand, once questioning about Church tradition was begun, others felt that the Church did not change rapidly enough. For these members even the new service was too traditional. Such members would choose instead to conduct their improvised services, led by a progressive priest. Meeting outside the Church, they would discuss inspirational readings and substitute a simple ceremony for the Mass, using ordinary bread and wine.

The new freedom unleashed in the Church raised the problem of how to handle freedom and what its limits should be. Once again the old question of the extent of authority the Pope should exert was revived, now reformulated in twentieth-century terms. Many had accepted the autocratic nature of the Church hierarchy, which imposed decisions from above, as the way things should be. The Vatican Council's directive for the Pope to share the decision-making process with bishops, bishops with priests, and priests with laity, however, caused this procedure to be reassessed. The Council simply advised the Pope to consult. He still maintained absolute authority and freedom to do so or not as he wished. Two points of view on papal authority emerged. Conservatives clung to the idea of the Church as a monarchical state that imposed conformity from above. Others, however, saw the Church as a collective of spiritual communities and wanted more guidance toward collaborative decisions than coercion from above. In general, the more progressive of these thinkers felt the Council had not gone far enough. Instead of merely possible consultation, they wanted all levels of church members to have ensured participation in Church decisions. Such a policy was endorsed by the prestigious Canon Law Society of America in 1966. In Holland, where the reforms of Vatican II were instituted most quickly, the bishops set up the National Pastoral Council with delegates elected by the people at large, who also often originated proposals for debate.

The question of papal authority came to a head in 1968 when Pope Paul VI issued an encylical, *Humanae Vitae*, condemning all forms of artificial birth control. The overwhelming majority of bishops on a special commission set up to study the problem favored a statement supporting birth control. The reason they did so was that the example of 80 percent of American Catholics disregarding the prohibition against artificial birth control represented a general trend. Thus, the Pope's minority position became an assertion of papal authority. The result was increasingly vocal criticism of the Pope for not taking majority sentiment into account. Since, in the spirit of the sixties, the more radical members of the Church often expressed their dissenting opinions publicly, through demonstrations, sit-ins, or statements picked up by a world press, many expected a confrontation at the Second Synod of Bishops held in 1969. Instead, however, the conservatives displayed a clear upper hand. The bishops simply agreed that collegiality would take more time to work out. They reaffirmed the Pope's complete freedom to act on his own, and merely expressed the hope that he would indeed seek out their collaboration. The clear tendency for the Vatican to keep bishops in line since that time is seen in acts such as that forbidding the continuation of the democratically elected Dutch National Pastoral Council.

One result of the twentieth-century scrutiny of the question of authority in the Church has been a re-emphasis on personal moral responsibility and individual conscience. The traditional authoritarian structure of the Church created a climate that fostered lay obedience to the external directives of bishops, priests, and confessors. The new questioning of this structure, however, emphasized the way traditions of the Church had developed in specific historical contexts. This new emphasis transformed the old idea of Christian morality based on absolute and unchanging values. Instead, it acknowledged the way Christian morality is rooted in individual and personal choices made among competing and even conflicting human values. The questioning helped many see that the Church hierarchy not only did not have all the answers, but that the answers had to be found anew by each person. The new personalism changed the focus from asking the Church to provide absolute answers, to seeking to be led in a dialogue between a member's own situation and that of a community of Christian believers, both past and present, represented by the teachings of the Church. The awareness of the historical nature of the Church also made many who faulted the Church for lack of moral leadership in such issues as war, peace, and racism in the past, more eager to take responsibility for such moral decisions themselves.

Naturally there has been a problem of finding the right balance between the traditionalist and personalist positions on Catholic morality. In general, however, the personalists are concerned to adapt traditional moral teaching to the complexities of modern life, and to changing developments in contemporary knowledge about human nature. One of the sharpest battlegrounds for this kind of debate has been the traditional prohibition of divorce. While both sides want to continue the emphasis on marriage for Catholics as a divine sacrament and lifelong commitment, some priests and theologians have questioned the wisdom and even the historical basis of the absolute nature of the prohibition. According to Catholic law even the Pope cannot dissolve a marriage. While the Church can allow a separation, it will allow remarriage only if one partner dies. In reality, however, many otherwise good practicing Catholics do get divorced and remarry without the sanction of the Church. The more progressive Church laity members and hierarchy advocate a more flexible policy on divorce which would take the reality of broken marriages in modern life more closely into account. Some priests, feeling that the rigid policy only serves to worsen an already difficult situation, give personal sanction to second marriages. Others do so to prevent otherwise observant Catholics from leaving the Church. The most extreme, however, advocate that the Church leave the entire area of marriage and divorce to the secular courts. In the issue of divorce, as of birth control, many Catholics are learning both to live with conflicting opinions within the Church and to follow their own dictates.

The new emphasis on the historical context of Church tradition has also created a question of Church doctrine. The focus is no longer in the unchangeable nature of the expressions of doctrine, but on the way they are historically conditioned responses to questions raised by a particular time. Such theologians as M.C. Chenu (b. 1895), Henri de Lubac (b. 1896), Jean Danielou (d. 1974), Teilhard de Chardin (d. 1955), and E. Schillebeeckx (b. 1896) all sought to relate doctrine and faith to the changing context of cultures and civilizations. The traditional Neo-Scholastic view of revelation as the transmission of definite fixed concepts was changed to the idea of revelation as a personal self-disclosure by which God communicates in a historical dialogue. In this new view, every formulation is simply a beginning which does not exhaust the truth. In fact, every era must redefine the truth in its own way.

This new theology was expressed by the *Dutch New Cathechism*, which appeared in 1966. As in all other reforms, however, for many the new theology was too much too soon. The Pope appointed a commission of cardinals to examine the *New Cathechism*. Their report in 1968 found such doctrines as original sin, eucharistic sacrifice, virginal conception of Mary, infallibility, and the source of authority in the Church inadequately explained. Consequently, after much negotiation, a compromise amendment to the *New Cathechism* was published as an appendix.

Alarmed by the unprecedented flurry of theological

speculation, the more traditional theologians called for a new *Syllabus of Errors* at the first Synod of 1967. Once again, however, a compromise between conservatives and progressives set up an international commission of theologians to help the Holy See deal with doctrinal confusion instead. Stronger action was taken against Hans Kung's call to discard the notion of papal infallibility altogether, on the grounds that historical and biblical research disproved any evidence of it. The *Declaration Against Certain Errors of the Present Day*, issued in 1973 by the Sacred Congregation for the Doctrine of Faith, insisted on traditional Catholic teaching on the infallibility of the Church and the Pope. It admitted that history influences the expression of doctrine, but denied dogmatic relativism, the notion that dogmas are only a series of approximations, always falling short of the truth. It repeated the traditional assertion that guarantees immunity from error to the Pope and bishops when they define Church doctrine.

The Vatican also issued a call for Kung to come to Rome for an official examination of the orthodoxy of his views. The changing attitude toward authority in the Church can be seen in the support of Kung's refusal to be examined by a petition calling for a change in Rome's procedure for dealing with theologians who do not agree with official doctrine.

One of the most visible manifestations of what some have perceived as a crisis in the authority of the Church after Vatican II can be seen in the challenge to adapt the role of the clergy to contemporary needs. As in previous eras of reform, questioning the need for priestly celibacy has been revived. The Scriptural foundations of celibacy have been challenged. Moreover, the Vatican directive to see the Church as a community of the faithful in which laity and priests play a more equal role has lent support to the idea that celibacy is a concept whose usefulness is past. As in the Lutheran reformation, many have left the priesthood to marry, while others have endorsed marriage as a means of carrying on a more active ministry. Many espouse a priesthood of personal commitment whose effectiveness might be enhanced by the priest's sharing the married situation of the majority of parishioners.

The greatest disruption has occurred among the religious orders. There, adaptation to a secularized world has been dramatized by exchanging the traditional distinctive priestly garb of nuns and monks for ordinary street clothes. In some cases orders have been torn apart by disagreements between conservative upholders of the status quo and those who endorse a more radical change. The decade after the Vatican Council saw many leave the enclosed orders. The reasons varied. In general, however, many no longer could support the rules of obediency and celibacy. A great many endorsed a more active social responsibility. As was the case with other issues, many bishops were sympathetic to adapting the rules of celibacy in order to ensure that those who were otherwise observant Catholics would be able to live with their conscience within the Church.

Questioning the meaning and extent of Catholic social action and the way it should be enacted reveals the struggle of the clergy and laity to come to terms with the relationship between individual conscience and collective action in a changing world. In *Mater et Magister,* issued in 1961 to commemorate the seventieth anniversary of *Rerum Novarum,* Pope John expressed the desire of the Church for the whole world to address the problems of social justice in a changing world. But it was in *Pacem in Terris*, just before he died, that Pope John specifically pointed to the need for the individual conscience to attend to correcting racial injustice and imperialism in order to attain world peace. In the United States the emphasis on correcting economic injustice had taken priority over the correction of racial injustice. During the thirties the lay Catholic Workers Movement and the Catholic Interracial Council did what they could to attack racist attitudes, but only after the experience of the Second World War did a number of Catholic bishops actively work against segregation. The civil rights movement of the late fifties and sixties, however, saw a few radical activist priests and nuns begin to join marches, protests, sit-ins, and voter registration drives to fight for civil rights.

The coming of age of the American Catholic Church during the sixties could be seen in its reaction to the morality of the Vietnam War. At issue was the Catholic concept of the "just war," defined as a war fought by a proper authority for a just cause. This concept made it morally indefensible for Catholics to become conscientious objectors during the late fifties. In 1965, however, undoubtedly emboldened by the "arrival" of the Catholic Church signified by the election of President Kennedy and the era of Pope John XXIII, two lone Catholic priests, Daniel and Philip Berrigan, signed a declaration of conscience pleading total noncooperation with the United States policy of escalating the war. The following year Cardinal Spellman presented the bishops' position by announcing his support for his country, right or wrong. In contrast, the growth of the

Catholic Peace Fellowship showed increasing lay feeling that the war was wrong. A similar stand against
violence was taken by the Church hierarchy in Ireland
in 1969. Although to little avail, it denounced the terrorist exchanges with British Protestants that had
erupted from the demand for Catholic civil rights in
Northern Ireland. In 1967 Pope Paul set up the Pontifical Commission for Justice and Peace to explore the
problems of war. By 1971 the American bishops urged
an end to U.S. involvement in the Vietnam War. And by
the time the Commission was made permanent in 1974,
the Church had reversed its official attitude, making it
morally acceptable for Catholics to declare con-
scientious-objector status.

Pope Paul's own contribution to broadening social
justice, a concern he had demonstrated by his efforts
for workers as Archbishop of Milan, came with his
encyclical *Populorum Progressio* in 1967. Focusing on
the needs of the underdeveloped countries, he asserted
the priority of human dignity and need over such
motives as profit, competition, and private ownership.
He reminded those in control of wealth and power of
the need for a redistribution of resources that was more
helpful than mere financial aid, something he was trying to achieve by an unpopular realignment of Vatican
wealth as well. Although the encyclical specifically
condemned revolution as violence which begets violence and injustice, it marked an important shift by the
Church in awareness of the political nature of its mission for social justice. This shift in awareness indicated
by the encyclical's recognition of the clear harm to the
common good from the denial of fundamental human

rights involved in prolonged tyranny is credited with influencing political activism in Latin America.

In Latin America, where 92 percent of the 310 million people are Catholic, since at least the thirties the Catholic Christian Democratic party intended to be associated with land reform, education, and other development programs for the masses. However, there was a separation for many between religious and political action. As successive Latin American countries became overrun by oppressive military regimes, many clergy in Latin America began to feel that the Catholic Church was the only institution that could stand up to dictators. Emboldened by Pope Paul's encyclical, in a historic meeting of Latin American bishops at Medellin, Colombia, in 1968, the bishops from such countries as Brazil, Chile, and Ecuador publicly denounced the violations of human rights perpetrated by their military regimes, and voiced their support for the oppressed poor. While many other older, conservative members of the clergy often continued to tolerate or even openly support military regimes, increasingly many younger priests denounced this behavior. They tended to interpret Vatican II and Paul VI's encyclical as an endorsement of their growing commitment to liberation theology. Fundamental to such works as *A Theology of Liberation* (1971), by Gustavo Gutierrez of Peru, is the idea that the Church must not only take a clear stand *against* social injustice, but that it must also take a clear stand *for* justice by actively participating in the revolutionary process seeking to abolish injustice and build a better order. In 1971 Pope Paul's Apostolic letter, *Octogesima Adveniens* (Call to Action), seemed to endorse this view in its call for a just and necessary transformation of society through collective action. And by 1977 Latin American activist priests had received some support from their activist American counterparts.

A relatively new issue in the concern to adapt the Catholic clergy to a changing world has been the movement to admit women into the secular ministry. This issue, arising out of the general western movement of the 1960s calling for a reevaluation of women's unequal status in comparison with men, has not yet spread to the Eastern communities. The movement has been reinforced from within the Church by its own reevaluation of history and by its recovery of an understanding of the historical Church as a whole people of God. Vatican II supported the call for public recognition of women's dignity in Pope John XXIII's encyclical *Pacem in Terris* of 1963. In 1971 there was a call within the Church for action to end discrimination against women in many countries. And the Third Bishops' Synod urged women to share responsibility and participate in the communal life of the Church and society.

Nevertheless, in 1972 women were explicitly excluded from the new lay ministries of lector and acolyte. A Pontifical Biblical Commission reported that it could find no support for exclusion of women from ordained priesthood on the basis of the Bible alone. The Canon Law Society, the Catholic Theological Society of America, and the Leadership Conference of Women Religious all favor the admission of women. They argue that nothing in the Bible excludes women, that women served as deaconesses in the past, and that the exclusion of women violates human dignity. On the other hand, those against the admission of women argue that ordination is not a right, that tradition opposes the admission of women, and that priests must represent Christ physically as well as spiritually. The prevailing conservative tendency to pull back from some of the more progressive endorsements of Vatican II can be seen by the statement opposing admission of women on those grounds in the 1976 Vatican Declaration on the *Question of Admission of Women to the Ministerial Priesthood.*

In 1978 Pope Paul VI died. The world was stunned when his successor, Pope John Paul I, known as the gentle, smiling Pope, lived only thirty-three days after the simple ceremony of installation he had insisted on rather than a coronation. The subsequent election of the Polish Cardinal Karol Wojtyla on October 16, 1978, was triply historic. At fifty-eight he was the youngest Pope since Pio Nono in 1846, the first non-Italian Pope since 1522, and the first ever to come from a Slavic nation. Like his predecessor, the new Pope also broke with tradition and declined a coronation. He celebrated the pontifical Mass in St. Peter's Square, where it was enjoyed not only by the 250,000 who thronged the square, but also by the millions who watched the live television broadcast throughout the world. The choice of this Pope from a Communist-ruled country was symbolic of the power of the Church not merely to survive but to flourish, even in the midst of an increasingly secular world. For in Poland, where paradoxically the majority (including Communist Party members) are overwhelmingly Catholic, the Church has been a powerful historical and patriotic as well as spiritual force.

The world applauded the choice of this former Archbishop of Krakow. Pope John Paul II's unique combination of personal qualities, training, and experience made him especially suited to take on the leadership of the Church at this time. The man who has been a physical laborer, sportsman, actor, professor, and writer is above all a lover of people, with a special commitment to the oppressed, a commitment that is especially meaningful since this Pope has experienced oppression. All his initial university studies took place at the outbreak of the Second World War when the Polish academic community was forced underground. He experienced the Nazis not only closing Jagellonian University in Krakow where he was enrolled, but sending most academics off to concentration camps. During this period he was also forced to work as a laborer in the mines. Meanwhile he continued his studies, joining extracurricular drama and literary groups as well. He combined his experiences by working to improve not only labor conditions for his fellow workers, but cultural, recreational, and spiritual facilities as well.

Some feel the young Pope's moral indignation over Nazi behavior during the occupation of Poland was instrumental in his decision to become a priest in 1942, at the age of twenty-two. During this period the Nazis listed him as an undesirable for his anti-Nazi activities, which included personally helping Jewish families escape. At any rate, shortly after his father's death, the young student activist sacrificed the study of Polish language and literature, which he loved, to enroll in an underground seminary. When he was ordained priest in 1946, the Stalinist desire to suppress religion and impose atheism on Poland meant that many priests were being arrested and held, including the Primate of Poland, Cardinal Wyszynski. Despite these adverse conditions, the Pope's career shone with many firsts. In 1958 he became Poland's youngest bishop. By 1963 he was Archbishop of Krakow, and in 1967 he became the second youngest living cardinal. Underground resistance to oppression as a student became refusal to be silent as leader of the Polish Church. In 1968 Cardinal Wojtyla spoke out against the official antisemitic Communist policy in Poland, and opposed further expulsion from their homeland of the Jews left in Poland after the Holocaust.

As a leader in the postwar Polish Church, the Pope acquired a reputation for his skill in dealing with the Communist state. Considering the enemy the new religious atheism and agnosticism, rather than the political party, he discouraged militant anti-Communism. His sound knowledge of Marxism and respect for opposing ideas helped Poland become a place of dialogue rather than confrontation between Church and state. Within this dialogue, the Pope spoke out for human dignity and freedom of belief, but also counselled Catholics to resist precipitating further strife.

The Polish Pope honored all three previous Popes by choosing to continue their names as John Paul II. The choice has proved extremely apt. Pope John Paul II is dedicated to maintaining the simplicity in the papacy emphasized by John Paul I. Like Pope John XXIII, he is an exceptionally charismatic man of the people, devoted to the role of Pope as teacher of the faith and servant of the faithful. Like Pope Paul VI, he is committed to the spirit of reform of Vatican II, but at the same time sees the need to assert strong papal authority.

John Paul II was an active participant in the sessions of Vatican II, where his strong voice on behalf of human dignity, religious freedom, and ecumenism helped shape the policy of reform. His book *The Foundations of Renewal* (1970), which explained the significance of Vatican II, helped promote an understanding of its work. He acted to implement the new teachings in Poland in yet another way by setting up a council composed of both clergy and laity to study specific issues and institute policy in each parish church. Like Pope Paul, he readily endorsed such changes as vernacular mass and Christian reunification. As a professor and leader in the Polish Church, John Paul II encouraged such experiments as "Jesus Christ Superstar" and religious retreats that combined hiking and canoeing with religious conversation. But like Pope Paul VI, John Paul also sees the need to hold the line, reverting to traditional policy on birth control, abortion, celibacy, and divorce, and even seeking a return to traditional religious dress.

Like his predecessor as well, the Polish Pope has seen the need for a strong papal authority and the assertion of the limits of reform. The effect of his conservative theological stand became clear just before Christmas of 1979. Under John Paul's leadership the Vatican declared that Hans Kung could no longer be considered a Catholic theologian and teacher. It also called Dutch theologian Edward Schillebeeckx to Rome to be questioned about the emphasis on the human person rather than the divine Christ, in his book *Jesus: An Experiment in Christology.*

Perhaps the most public assertion of John Paul's hard line on theological dissent came in October 1979 during his tour of the United States. The focus of the dissent was the Vatican's decision against allowing Catholic women to be ordained as priests, but the issue was the much broader one of the role of women in the Church. Although in Philadelphia traditionalists had cheered the Pope's reaffirmation of the Church's stand against ordination of women, clerical groups such as Priests for Equality and a Boston nuns' organization as well as Catholic Advocates for Equality, composed of both clergy and laity all called for priests and nuns to boycott the Pope's Mass because women were not asked to serve Communion. The most dramatic expression of the dissatisfaction of religious groups, however, was the unexpected public request of Sister Theresa Kane, president of the Leadership Conference of Women Religious, an official church organization of American nuns, for Pope John Paul to be open and responsive to women's desire to serve the Church as fully participating members.

Declining to respond directly, the Pope affirmed his earlier position, and urged the five thousand nuns present, roughly one-third in secular clothes, to emulate the femininity of the Virgin Mary and to revert to traditional dress. Speaking to a group of Italian nuns a week later, the Pope again asserted that the role the Church assigns to religious women is that of sensible and illuminated mothers rather than priests, and urged them to accept this role meekly and without bitterness, and to revert to traditional dress.

John Paul's conservative theological stand is often partially explained by the unique situation of the Polish Church. The strength of that Church in its struggle to survive in the midst of imposed atheism has lain in its adherence to tradition and obedience to Rome. But liberals argue that in its struggle the Polish Church has been insulated from the different temptations of secularism in such free and pluralistic western societies as the Netherlands and the United States. They assert that different pressures in these countries point to different needs. In 1979, for example, average weekly church attendance in the United States had fallen among Catholics from 71 percent in 1964 to 52 percent. About 12 million of the nation's 49.6 million Catholics had become inactive, "unchurched," believers. In addition, surveys found a rise in Catholics favoring ordination of women from 29 percent in 1974 to 40 percent. That increased percentage indicated both a heightened awareness of the problem as symptomatic of a larger insensitivity to the unequal position of women in the Church, and a declining number of clerics. In 1979 the number of candidates for ordination decreased to 13,960, one third the candidates of 1965; the number of American nuns fell from a peak of 181,431 in 1966 to 128,378; and an estimated 10,000 American priests left the Church, many of them because of the persistence of the celibacy requirement. Also in 1979 a thousand-member national organization, the Association for the Rights of the Catholic Church, issued a position paper asserting the position that not only is dialogue in the

Church fundamental, but that Catholics have the right and at times the obligation to dissent. In these situations, liberals argue, the strong authority which is necessary for survival in the Polish Church is not a solution, but simply aggravates the problems of the Dutch and American Church.

Others explain John Paul's authoritarianism as aimed at the Church of the twenty-first century, which will no longer be composed predominantly of Westerners. In fact, while 85 percent of Christianity lived in the West in 1900, only 42 percent will be living in the West by A.D.2000. The rest, including 70 percent of all Catholics, will be living in the Third World countries of Asia, Africa, and Latin America.

The Pope has also asserted papal authority to curb the growing trend for political activism among Catholic priests. His caution against political involvement to priests during his tour of Mexico in 1979 was particularly disappointing to many clergy in Latin America. In the Pope's view, the role of the Church is to heal division, not to encourage further factions in society or within the Church. Essentially, he has asked priests to make spiritual values rise above politics. He has counselled a separation of spheres of action, encouraging the laity to work for social justice in the political sphere and the clergy to enact social justice through the words of the Gospel.

For adherents of liberation theology, however, religion cannot be separated from the inherently political nature of all human institutions. They argue that in a radically divided world the Church must struggle against the causes of division. It can enact the words of the Gospel only by accepting its dual responsibilities to recognize its own participation in injustice and to work to create change.

Such traditionally activist priests as the Jesuits and the Maryknollers, an American missionary group established in 1911, claim that the Pope and conservative bishops do not understand the different needs of the Latin American church, where poverty rather than atheism is the enemy. In 1981 when the Jesuit Superior general suffered a serious stroke, however, the Pope asserted his authority over the Jesuits by substituting his own choice of an interim leader over that of the Jesuits. After receiving 5,000 letters in protest from Jesuit leaders, at a meeting in Rome, the Pope explained that his appointment was temporary and that an election among the Jesuits would take place in 1983. However, he also counselled that there was no longer any room for deviation. He counselled greater knowledge of traditional doctrine, and he restricted traditional Jesuit independence from bishops—who often disagree with Jesuit political activism—by broadening the definition of Jesuit direct obedience to himself to make it include working in close union and collaboration with his bishops.

Both theology and pragmatics were probably involved. Throughout history activist priests have been criticized and harassed by Latin American landowners and government. In 1976 the Ecuadorian military government arrested thirty-seven clergy, including thirteen bishops and archbishops meeting to discuss Church involvement in the struggle against social injustice. The fate of increasingly activist Maryknollers, who work with the poor under the direct supervision of bishops, points to worsening dangers. In 1980 two

Maryknoll nuns and two other missionaries were murdered by the El Salvador government. Shortly after-
wards all Maryknollers were requested to leave El Salvador, more were expelled from the Phillipines,
accused of fomenting political unrest and portraying
Jesus as a rebel, and no further Maryknollers were
allowed in the Honduras. No gospel can be enacted by
priests who are murdered, expelled, or denied further
entry into Latin America.

The Pope then sees the assertion of papal authority in
Latin America as important for survival. He also sees a
leadership that asserts strong doctrinal continuity as
important for the different needs of the Afro-Asian
block, which the Church explicitly recognized through
the Bishops' Synod of 1974 as needing to cultivate a
distinctive Catholicism expressing the unique Asian
and African cultural heritages. Thus, the Pope's assertion of authority is seen as an expression of his sense of
the leadership necessary to maintain the strength of
Catholicism for the future, to provide the unifying factor for a world which somehow needs to blend centralized leadership with individualized manifestations
of the same basic faith.

John Paul's reign has been marked by the strength of
the leadership he has striven to provide. From the beginning of his reign, the first Polish Pope worked hard
to bring the Church to the people. Visiting twenty-one
countries on five continents, Africa, Asia, North and
South America, and Europe, in his first two and a-half
years established the Pope's nickname of the "per-
ipatetic Pope." His reign has been punctuated by a
succession of historic first occasions for such countries
as Poland, Mexico, Ireland, England, and Argentina to

receive a visit from a ruling Pope. The unprecedented crowds of people throughout the world who have seen this Pope have been struck by the combination of youthful energy, good spirits, humility, and simple kindness expressed in his words and deeds.

John Paul has also worked hard to provide leadership for the world. Like his predecessors, he has continued to promote the idea of Christian religious unity as a model for attaining universal peace. His 1979 visit to the Patriarch of the Eastern Orthodox Church in Istanbul set in motion talks on the reunification of the Orthodox and Roman Churches. The meeting of the Orthodox-Catholic joint commission in June 1982 was the second meeting to discuss the possibility of healing the separation between the two Churches in twenty years, after a break of four centuries. The Pope's visit to Germany in 1980 reopened a similar dialogue with the Lutheran Church. The strongest possibility for reunification comes from the Anglican Church. A joint commission of both the Anglican and Catholic Churches agreed in 1981 on the concept of a single head for both Churches in Rome, with the title Bishop of Rome, rather than Pope. The union that is envisaged would not be an absorption of the Anglican into the Catholic Church, but a confederation of distinct, spiritually united sister Churches. The Anglicans agreed that the Bishop of Rome could, under certain conditions, intervene in local matters, and could on occasion speak on behalf of the Church. But they insisted that before the utterances could be accepted as those of the Church, they would have to reflect the consent of the fellow bishops representing the Church as a whole.

In fact while Pope Paul was the pilgrim Pope, John

Paul has become the pilgrim of difficult moments. Using such vehicles of modern technology as the papal jet, "Shepherd I," he has taken his battle against materialism and violence to the people. His presence in the midst of violence and oppression has been an impressive reinforcement to his words. In 1979 during his historic trip to Northern Ireland, ripped apart by fierce battles between Protestants and Catholics, the Pope's presence and diplomacy were an attempt to inspire both sides to see that the Church wishes above all for violence on both sides to end. As he continued that journey, the Pope's presence in Mexico at the Latin American bishops' conference at Puebla was proof of his shared concern for the poor, as was his appeal to the wealthy in the United States to demonstrate their concern for justice and poverty by a more equal distribution of their wealth.

Perhaps inevitably, the Pope's concern to be available to his people contributed to his own encounter with violence. In Rome the Pope moved the general papal audiences, traditionally held inside St. Peter's Basilica, outside into Vatican Square. He also changed the tradition of being carried on a chair to being driven through the crowds in an open-air jeep, affectionately known as the Popemobile. During one of these audiences in May 1981 the bullet of a Turkish terrorist struck and seriously wounded the Pontiff in a failed assassination attempt. The horror was almost relived again exactly one year later. In May 1982 a second assassin lunged at the Pope, this time with a bayonet as John Paul was about to give thanks to Our Lady of Fatima in Portugal for his recovery from the first attempt. These encounters with death intensified the sense of the Pope as a human being that a stunned world had already felt. They also brought forcefully home what appears to be an intensification of violence since the times when Pope John could wander through Rome unscathed. The Pope, however, remained undaunted from his mission of showing the leadership the Church could provide for an increasingly troubled world.

One month later, in June 1982, the Pope became the first Roman Pontiff to set foot on British soil in four hundred years, carrying out a planned visit to Britain to cement agreement between the Anglican and Catholic Churches. His decision not to cancel the visit when Britain, which is only 13 percent Catholic, became plunged into war over the Falkland Islands with Argentina, which is 92 percent Catholic, emphasized the priority of Christian unity over temporary national disputes. The point was further underscored just before the Pope left Rome, by a Vatican Mass jointly celebrated by British and Argentine cardinals who exchanged a kiss of peace and issued a joint plea for an end to bloodshed. During the Pope's historic six-day visit to England, Scotland, and Wales, the possibility for healing the four-century split was dramatized by the Pope's own joint prayer service with the Archbishop of Canterbury and Anglican primates flown in from four continents. The historic first occasion for a Pope to worship in the great Anglican Canterbury Cathedral was marked by the presence of the Canterbury Gospels given to the first Archbishop of Canterbury by Pope Gregory I in 597, when the Church was one. Prospects for further reunification of the Church were enlarged by the Pope's meetings with representatives of the Scottish and Welsh Protestant Churches for the first time on their own soil.

Throughout his trip, the Pope's commitment to providing moral leadership in the face of division and danger greatly enhanced papal prestige. The grace with which the Pope blessed religious dissidents who turned out was heightened by the knowledge of the physical dangers he continued to risk, despite the security features built into his new Popemobiles.

The Pope's moral leadership was further affirmed when he balanced his British visit by becoming the first Pope to touch Argentine soil as well, seven days later. The decision itself revealed the strength of the desire of the Church for peace and neutrality. These concerns outweighed an earlier decision to withhold a visit to the Argentine because of its refusal to accept the terms of papal arbitration in its dispute with Chile. In Catholic Argentina the Pope brought the same plea to replace patriotism with piety that he had brought to Protestant Britain. He urged prayers for victims of both sides and counselled consideration of the absurd and unjust nature of all wars.

Pope John Paul's travels on behalf of lived Christian morality have been manifestations of the courage of his deeply felt convictions. Everywhere, the Pope speaks powerfully on behalf of human dignity, social justice, and peace. His hugging babies, speaking to special rallies for the young, singing popular songs, and joking about himself all reveal his deep feeling for people. But gestures such as his kneeling down to prevent the eighty-four-year-old American Bishop Fulton Sheen from kneeling to him, and leaving his own gold cardinal's ring as a donation to a small local church in Brazil especially bring Christian charity to life. The Pope's leadership has provided an example to his priests of the way spiritual values can rise above political concerns. That leadership has also provided the world with a model for possible peace.

Bibliography

Saint Augustine. *The City of God*. Trans. Marcus Dods. New York: Modern Library, 1950.

————. *The Confessions*. Trans. R. S. Pine-Coffin. Baltimore, Md.: Penguin Books, 1961.

Berrigan, Philip. *Prison Journals of a Priest Revolutionary*. New York: Ballantine Books, 1970.

Blazynski, George. *Pope John Paul II*. New York: Dell Publishing Company, 1970.

Bokenkotter, Thomas. *A Concise History of the Catholic Church*. Garden City, New York: Doubleday & Company, 1977.

Chadwick, Henry. *The Early Church, Pelican History of the Church*, Vol. 1. New York: Penguin Books, 1967.

Cragg, Gerald R. *The Church in the Age of Reason 1648–1789*. New York: Atheneum, 1961.

Daly, Mary. *Beyond God the Father: Towards a Philosophy of Women's Liberation*. Boston: Beacon Press, 1973.

————. *The Church and the Second Sex*. New York: Harper & Row Publishers, Inc., 1975.

Deanesly, Margaret. *A History of the Medieval Church 590–1500*. London: Methuen & Co., Ltd., 1954.

Dolan, John P. *Catholicism: An Historical Survey*. Woodbury, New York: Barron's Educational Series, 1968.

Dubnov, Simon. *History of the Jews: From the Beginning to Early Christianity*. Vol. 1. Trans. Moshe Spiegel. New York: Thomas Yseloff, 1967.

Enslin, Morton Scott. *Christian Beginnings*. Parts I & II. New York: Harper & Row Publishers, Inc., 1956.

Enslin, Morton Scott. *The Literature of the Christian Movement.*
Part III of Christian Beginnings. New York: Harper & Row
Publishers, Inc., 1956.

Hales, E. E. Y. *The Catholic Church in the Modern World, A Survey
From the French Revolution to the Present.* Garden City, New
York: Image Books, 1960.

Hatch Alden. *A Man Named John: The Life of Pope John XXIII.* New
York: Hawthorn Books, Incorporated, 1963.

Hughes, Paul. *A Popular History of the Catholic Church.* New York:
Macmillan Company, 1961.

Knowles, David. *The Evolution of Medieval Thought.* New York:
Vintage Books, 1962.

Leff, Gordon. *The Dissolution of the Medieval Outlook.* New York:
New York University Press, 1976.

———. *Medieval Thought: St. Augustine to Ockham.* Baltimore,
Md.: Penguin Books, 1958.

McBrien, Richard P. *Catholicism.* Vols. 1 and 2. Minneapolis:
Winston Press, 1980.

McKenzie, John L. *The Roman Catholic Church.* History of Religion
Series. New York: Holt, Rinehart and Winston, 1969.

May, Herbert G. and Bruce M. Metzger, ed. *The Oxford Annotated
Holy Bible,* Rev. Standard Version. New York: Oxford University
Press, 1962.

Meeks, Wayne A., ed. *The Writings of St. Paul.* A Norton Critical
Edition. New York: W. W. Norton & Company, Inc., 1972.

Neill, Stephen. *A History of Christian Missions.* New York: Penguin
Books, 1977.

Noel, Gerard. *The Anatomy of the Catholic Church.* Garden City,
New York: Doubleday & Company, Inc., 1980.

Pagels, Elaine. *The Gnostic Gospels.* New York: Vintage Books,
1981.

Pieper, Josef. *Scholasticism: Personalities and Problems of Medieval Philosophy.* New York: McGraw-Hill Book Company, 1964.

Reuther, Rosemary, and Eleanor McLaughlin, ed. *Women of Spirit:
Female Leadership in the Jewish and Christian Traditions.* New
York: Simon & Shuster, 1979.

Smith, Goldwin. *A History of England,* 2d ed. rev. New York:
Charles Scribners Sons, 1957.

Southern, R. W. *Western Society and the Church in the Middle
Ages.* The Pelican History of the Church. New York: Penguin
Books, 1970.

Swidler, Leonard. "Jesus was a Feminist," *The Catholic World* (Jan.
1971), 177–83.

Index

Abraham, and God's covenant, 10, 19, 29
Acton (Lord), 132–133, 135, 155; and *The Rambler*, 133
African Church, 42, 44, 48
Alexander V (Pope), 86
Alexander VI (Pope), 92
Alexander III (Pope), 68
Ambrose (Bishop of Milan), 44, 52; and Emperor Theodosius, 52
American Church, 115, 152–154, 193
apostles, 18–19, 29, 30, 32, 34, 36; authority of, 29, 30; the twelve, 29
Aquinas, Thomas, 78–79, 154; and Albertus Magnus, 78; and Jesuits, 104; and Thomism, 78–79, 154
Arianism, 39, 40, 47, 53, 55
Augustine, 42–49, 56, 94–95; and Augustinians, 76; and celibacy, 47–48; and *City of God*, 48; and *Confessions*, 42; and monasticism, 48; conversion of, 42, 44; influence of, on Church, 42–49
Augustus, Philip, 69–70, 83; and Pope Innocent III, 69–70
Avignon residency, 84–85, 87, 92, 93

Baltimore Councils, 144–145
Becket, Thomas à (Archbishop of Canterbury), 68
Benedict XV (Pope), 159–160
Benedictine monks, 57, 74–75
Benedict XIII (Pope), 86
Bible, 91; and Biblical Commission, 154, 156; and Church Fathers, 100; authority of, 100, 110–111; authority of, over the Church, 91, 100; historical criticism of, 155, 173
bishops, 33–35, 39, 47, 48, 52–53, 56, 61–62, 67, 117, 150, 175; and cathedral schools, 59; and election of Pope, 62; and National Pastoral Council, 177; and simony, 61; and Theatines, 100; election of, 62; Second Synod of, 178; submission of, to king, 61
Boniface VIII (Pope), 82–83; and *Cleris Laicos*, 83; and *Unam Sanctam*, 82
Brethren of the Common Life, 94, 99

Catholic, clergy, 37, 40; dioceses, 165; liturgy, 36–37, 42; missionary movement, 106; missions, 141; revival, 123; scholars, 155; schools, 146; tradition, 29, 56; *see also* Catholic Church; Catholicism; Church; Roman Catholic Church
Catholic Action League, 161, 166
Catholic Church, 9, 18–19, 25, 27, 32–34, 40, 42, 47–48, 79, 99, 100, 104, 109, 111, 161, 185, 192; and Gnosticism, 32–33; medieval, 78; roots of authority of, 18–19; *see also* Catholic; Catholicism; Church; Roman Catholic Church
Catholic Reformation, 101–103
Catholic University, 151–152
Catholic Workers Movement, 162, 183

203